UNITED

WE

STAND

ALSO BY ERIC WALTERS

Bi–focal
House Party
Boot Camp
Camp X–Fool's Gold
Sketches
We All Fall Down
Shattered
Laggan Lard Butts
Stuffed
Elixir
Triple Threat
Camp 30
Grind
The True Story of Santa Claus
Juice
Run
Overdrive
I've Got an Idea
Underdog
Death by Exposure
Royal Ransom
Off Season
Camp X
Road Trip
Tiger Town
The Bully Boys
Long Shot
Ricky
Tiger in Trouble

Hoop Crazy
Rebound
The Hydrofoil Mystery
Full Court Press
Caged Eagles
The Money Pit Mystery
Three on Three
Visions
Tiger by the Tail
Northern Exposures
War of the Eagles
Stranded
Trapped in Ice
Diamonds in the Rough
Stars
Stand Your Ground
Splat!
The Falls
In a Flash
The Pole
When Elephants Fight
La Voyageur
Safe as Houses
Alexandria of Africa
Tell Me Why
Special Edward
Black & White
Wounded

UNITED

WE

STAND

a novel by **ERIC WALTERS**

DOUBLEDAY CANADA

Doubleday Canada and colophon are trademarks.

LIBRARY AND ARCHIVES CANADA CATALOGUING IN PUBLICATION HAS
BEEN APPLIED FOR

ISBN: 978-0-385-66640-4

Printed and bound in the USA

Published in Canada by Doubleday Canada,
a division of Random House of Canada Limited

Visit Random House of Canada Limited's website: www.randomhouse.ca

10 9 8 7 6 5 4 3 2 1

UNITED

WE

STAND

CHAPTER
ONE

My eyes opened ever so slightly. The bed felt warm and soft, and all I wanted to do was sleep some more. But there was light coming through the window and I thought I really should get up . . . probably. I sat up and stretched and looked down at my hands. They were both cut, and there was a line of stitches extending from the palm of my left hand almost up to the wrist. My hand was throbbing. Then it all came back to me.

It was like some sort of bizarre dream—no, a night-mare—but I knew it was all real. There was the evidence, right there on my hands—the cuts, the gash that I got crawling through the debris and the dust storm and then scrambling away, unable to see or breathe, on all fours. I remembered thinking that I'd survived the plane crashing into the building, the explosion, the fire, the mad rush down the stairs, and the collapse of the building, only to die, suffocating, in the dust and debris.

I started to cough like I was still somewhere in that cloud of dust. There was something stuck in my throat. I continued to cough until I spat it out into my hand—thick, black phlegm. God knows what it was, but I figured almost anything could have been lining my throat and lungs. I wiped it on the side of the bedspread.

"Will!"

It was my mother. She was standing in my bedroom doorway. She looked so upset—she must have seen me wiping the gunk on the bedspread.

She burst into tears, rushed over, and threw her arms around me.

"I'm just . . . just so glad . . . you're okay," she sobbed.

"I'm fine . . . I'm good."

"Let me look at you."

She released her grip and leaned back so she could look me square in the eyes. She started crying again.

"I'm fine, honestly. You don't have to cry."

"Honey, these are tears of *joy*. I'm just so glad you're all right. And your hand. How is your hand?"

She held up my left hand and looked at the stitches. Even I had to admit that it did look nasty, like I'd been in a knife fight—and lost.

"It must hurt terribly," she said.

"Not really. It feels almost numb. It looks a lot worse than it is," I said. "Speaking of which . . . *you* look *awful*."

She laughed. I hadn't expected that.

"I haven't slept," she said. "The two of you were coughing so badly all night."

"We were? I didn't notice . . . I thought I slept right through."

"*You* did. But it kept me awake. I had to be awake anyway, though, to check on your father because of his concussion."

"Dad . . . is he okay?"

"He's saying that he's fine. Not that I know if I should believe him."

"I want to see him," I said as I yanked off the blankets and swung my feet to the floor. "Where is he?"

"He's in the den."

I climbed out of bed and stumbled slightly, my legs giving way under me. My mother reached out and took me by the arm to steady me. My legs were sore all over, particularly painful in a couple of spots, and I remembered then that my knees and legs were just as cut up and bruised as my hands.

"Let me help you," my mother offered.

I didn't argue. I felt like I needed her help. "I want to see Dad."

She led me out of the bedroom, through the kitchen, and toward the den. The door was slightly ajar and I could hear him—he was talking to somebody.

Gently I knocked on the door and pushed it open wider. He was standing by the window. He was alone, talking on the phone.

His face was all cut and bruised, and I was shocked at how swollen one side was. It hadn't been that swollen last night. His left arm was in a sling, and I knew underneath his shirt were three fractured ribs. If he was coughing all night he would have been in a lot of pain.

He saw us, gave a little smile that was distorted by the swelling, and motioned for us to come in. He continued his conversation.

"I know there will be some complications involved in transferring that amount of money," he said.

Unbelievable. Yesterday we'd both almost died and here he was doing business, like nothing had happened. I'd had some fleeting fantasy that somehow this would change his compulsion for working so hard, but I guess I was wrong. Business was business, and that would never—

"Hold on a second," he said into the phone.

He put the phone down on the desk and walked over and wrapped his arms around me, giving me a gigantic hug. Maybe something *had* changed. I hugged him back and he groaned—I'd forgotten about his ribs.

"Sorry."

"No need to apologize," he said. "Just good to have your arms around me."

I felt the same way.

He loosened his grip so he could look at me. "How you doing, kid?"

"I'm good."

"You don't seem so good."

"Look who's talking," I said.

He chuckled. "I guess you're right, but really, are you okay?"

"As okay as I can be. You?"

"I am now." He let go of me. "Sit down, this will just take a minute . . . It's important."

He picked up the phone again. "Listen, Suzie, I just want—"

"Suzie is okay!" I exclaimed.

My father smiled and nodded.

I hadn't even thought about her, or any of the other people in the office. Most of them would have gotten out, I thought, but not all of them . . . Some of those people would have died . . . So many people had died.

"You call Cam Peters back and you tell him I want one hundred thousand dollars deposited directly into an account I can use at my discretion. Tell him that is a direct order from me, and if he doesn't do it immediately I'll be paying him a visit myself, and I'm not half as pretty or polite as you."

She said something I couldn't hear and he laughed.

"Good. Good. So, I'll see you here right after lunch."

Hearing this phone call about money and knowing my father the way I did, I had a good idea what was happening. He was going to start working, today, from here. He didn't have an office—he didn't even have a building—but it was going to take more than the collapse of the World Trade Center to stop him from doing business.

"And, Suzie, thanks for everything. I'm just so glad you're . . . you're . . . you got out. You know I love you."

What was he saying? She was his assistant, his very young assistant, and he was saying all this right in front of—

"Suzie, you're like family to me, like a daughter," he said. "Now, are you sure you're okay to come here today? If you don't feel up to it I'll understand . . . Okay, at least promise me that you'll drive carefully."

He put the phone down and turned to us. "Suzie is going to help me. I have to try to contact everybody, all the people in the office. I have to know if everybody . . . if everybody is okay."

"They should be fine," I said. "They all left before we did, and we got out."

I'd been with my father—it was sort of like "take your kid to work" day at my school— in his office on the eighty-fifth floor, South Tower, of the World Trade Center. I'd been there when the first plane hit the North Tower. And my father wasn't just the boss in his own office; he was the fire warden for the floor. Right away he'd ordered everybody in his office—all one hundred people—to stop whatever they were doing and evacuate the building. He'd given that order before the second plane hit our tower.

"I know they all left before us," he said. "But what if some of them heard the P.A. announcement and decided to go back?"

Just after my father had chased everybody out of the office, and before that second plane hit our building, there had been an announcement over the P.A. saying that there was no danger, that people shouldn't evacuate the South Tower, and that they should go back to their offices.

"They wouldn't have done that . . . They wouldn't have gone back . . . would they?"

He shook his head. "I have no way of knowing for sure," he said, "but some of our traders get so focused on the deal that they'll look for any excuse to get back to the office and start working again."

I started to snicker.

"I know, I know, but I'm hoping to slow down myself."

"Like today?" I asked.

"No choice today, but from now on there'll be shorter hours, fewer evenings. You'll see."

"We'd like that, dear," my mother said. "But seeing is believing."

"Sometimes it's the other way around. *Believing* is seeing."

I sort of got what he was saying. We never would have got out of that building if we hadn't believed. I was willing to give him the benefit of the doubt.

"I think they were all out," I said. "We were for sure the last ones in your office after the plane hit the building. Nobody else was there then, and I can't imagine anybody coming back up *after* the plane hit."

"I'm just afraid for anyone who might have been *trying* to come back," he said. "Maybe someone was heading up the stairs and ended up on the one of the floors where the plane hit."

I hadn't thought about that. The floors a few below ours—seventy-nine and eighty and eighty-one—had been devastated. Anybody on those floors would have been killed instantly.

"And," my father continued, "the announcement said people could take the elevators. What if people listened to that?"

I'd seen what had happened to some of the elevators. The metal doors had been blown right off and the walls directly across scorched by flames. I'd also heard about elevators that had just plunged down the shafts, killing everybody.

"Suzie's coming over to help me find a new office and locate all our people. Together we're going to try to talk to everybody," my father said. "The only problem is that when we lost the office we also lost all the home addresses and phone numbers for everybody in the company, worldwide."

"You don't have a backup?" my mother questioned.

"All financial dealings were backed up in our other offices, but the personnel information for all our branches around the world was kept in our office." He shook his head slowly, his expression sad. "They thought that ours was the most secure site."

"So, how are you going to do it?" my mother asked. "How are you going to get in touch with everybody?"

"Suzie socializes with a couple of the women from the office, so she has their numbers. Bill Saunders is a member of my fitness club. We know where some people live and we'll go through phone books. We're hoping that every person we reach will have contacts that will help us reach somebody else."

"That makes sense," I said. "But why do you need the money . . . ? You know, the money you asked to be transferred to you?"

"The money is to secure a lease, rent some office equipment, put in phones and computers. We have to get the business up and running."

"But right away? Today?"

"I have an obligation to the people in my office to get them back to work as soon as possible. Most people are only one paycheck away from defaulting on their mortgages, from going into bankruptcy. With no money coming in this week, there are people who might be desperate. This way, I'll have enough to give advances, or maybe even loans. With what they've all gone through, the last thing our employees should have to worry about now is money." He paused. "They might also need the money for other things."

I gave him a questioning look. "Like what?"

He didn't answer right away. "I was thinking about medical costs, maybe even funeral expenses. We can only hope that's not the case."

We could hope. I just didn't know if that hope was realistic. Tens of thousands of people had been injured, and thousands killed. Some of them *could* have been from my father's office.

"They might also need to see counselors," my mother added.

"Counselors for what?" I asked.

"People who have gone through tragedy, through difficult or dangerous situations, can suffer from the after-effects," she said.

"I don't understand," I told her. "If you survived, you survived."

"It's called post-traumatic stress disorder," she explained. "I learned about it when I was training as a social worker, and they were talking about it on CNN this morning. They said this is going to affect not just the people who were in the towers and their families, but people everywhere across the country, even around the world."

"Now I'm really confused. People who weren't even there are going to suffer from this post-traumatic whatever stress thing?"

"Stress disorder. People will have anxiety attacks, will become depressed, have sleep problems . . . I certainly couldn't sleep last night," my mother said.

"Yeah, but you had a reason. You were watching Dad because of the concussion. Besides, you'd spent the day thinking that we were dead—we *were* there."

"Your mother is right," my father said. "This is going to have an effect on people everywhere. And more than that, it's going to change everything."

Maybe my thinking was still a bit fuzzy, but I wasn't getting it.

"This is something that's going to be a turning point in history," my father went on. "Everybody will remember where they were and what they were doing at the moment they heard about the attack."

"I know where *I* was," I said. "I was right there."

"Yes, but everybody who watched it on television will feel like they were there too. And what happened will have an impact that we can't even imagine yet," my father said.

"This country has been changed," my mother said. "We don't know what those changes are going to be yet, but nothing will be the same."

"Wait . . . I know that man," my father said. He was pointing to a television in the corner of the room. With the sound turned down I hadn't even noticed it was on, but I recognized the man on the screen.

A CNN reporter was interviewing a man from the engineering firm just down the hall, on the same floor as my father's office. I didn't even know his name, but I was amazed at how happy I was to see that he was alive. I looked around desperately for the remote, but it was nowhere to be seen, so I rushed over to the set and turned the sound up manually.

"Can you describe the trip down the stairs?" the female reporter asked him.

"At first it was sort of like a fire drill at school. Everybody was just joking around . . . It was light, you know, playful," he said. "You have to remember, at that point, we didn't know much about what had happened in the other building—all we knew was that it had been hit by a plane. And our building hadn't been hit yet."

"And after the second plane did hit your building?"

"To tell you the truth, at first we still didn't know exactly what had happened," he said. "Not really. But we hadn't made it very far down the stairs, and we knew we were probably only three or four floors below the point of impact by then. We felt it. A couple of people were knocked over, and then we felt the whole building shake, and the lights went out and the sprinklers came on and some of the panels fell off the wall. It wasn't a school fire drill any more."

"And you are an engineer," the reporter said.

"Yes, a structural engineer. My firm designs buildings, bridges, parking structures. We know about how to put a building up," he said.

"Or what it might take to bring one down," the reporter said.

"That too. When the building reacted to the impact and started to really sway, I had a pretty good idea that something major had happened. And then when I smelled the fuel it was pretty clear that it was another plane."

"That must have been terrifying."

"That's the strangest part. It wasn't terrifying because it was just so . . . so . . . unreal."

"I can only imagine. And what was it like going down after that?"

"It suddenly got much more crowded, but it was really, really orderly. People were friendly, offering encouragement, helping other people."

"We've heard the same from other witnesses. It was as though this terrible event somehow brought out the very best in people."

"I guess the fact that nobody knew what was about to happen helped. If people had known how close we were to the collapse of the building, then panic would have set in, I think."

"As a structural engineer, you must have considered that possibility."

He shook his head. "As a structural engineer I didn't think there was a *chance* of it happening. Those buildings were *made* to sustain an airplane crash. I just assumed that the worst had passed. The plane had hit the tower and the building had absorbed the force. I thought it was simply a case of containing the fire. That was all."

"I guess perhaps ignorance was bliss."

"That's the strangest thing," he said. "My girlfriend was watching TV in her office uptown, and she knew more than we knew. People halfway around the world who were watching on TV knew more about what was happening than those of us in the building. I didn't know anything about the plane that hit the Pentagon, or about the fourth plane that was brought down in Pennsylvania."

My father and I hadn't heard about the other planes either, of course—not until we were being treated, stitched up, in the mobile hospital.

"Were there any people in your office who didn't . . . didn't make it?" the reporter asked.

"No. Everybody got out. We stayed as a group all the way out and onto the street. We were two blocks away by the time the South Tower collapsed. We were so incredibly fortunate that we left when we did."

The reporter turned toward the camera. "There were very few people above the floors where the impact occurred who survived. Mr. Johnston's—"

"Please, call me Dennis," the man said, and smiled.

"Certainly. Dennis's office was located on the eighty-fifth floor, and his survival was based on the fact that he made the decision to evacuate immediately after the first plane hit the North Tower."

"It really wasn't our decision," he said. "We left only because of the fire warden on our floor."

I turned to my dad. "That's you!"

He smiled and nodded.

"I don't even know his name," Mr. Johnston said. "I think it was John . . . John something."

"Fuller," I said to the TV.

"My hero," my mother said, and she reached out and grabbed my father's hand.

"Nothing heroic. I was just doing what a fire warden is supposed to do."

I thought back to how I'd wanted to leave right away, get out of the building, but my father had insisted on both making sure that all the employees from his office left and trying to get everybody from the entire floor to evacuate. The first place we'd gone to was the office where Mr. Johnston—Dennis—worked. He and the other staff had listened, closed up the offices, and left right away. Thank goodness they'd made it down before the second plane hit.

One of the other offices had not been so cooperative or friendly. My father had tried to convince the employees, tried ordering them to leave, but they had just refused. And then, when that stupid announcement came over the P.A. telling people not to evacuate, to go back to their offices, there was no chance of their listening to him any more. The boss there—some snotty little guy in a rumpled suit—ordered them back to work and pretty well tossed us out of their office. They went back to their phones and computers, trying to close another deal, make some more money. They were probably all dead now. That thought sent a shiver down my spine. They were all gone because they wouldn't listen to my father, and that guy on the TV and all his co-workers were alive because they did. What an unbelievable thought.

"That fire warden is the reason I'm alive," Mr. Johnston continued, "the reason *all* of us in our office are alive. I'd like to meet him, shake his hand, and thank him for what he did." He suddenly looked sad. "But I don't know if he . . . if he . . . He was still there on the floor when we left."

"And you don't know if he made it."

Mr. Johnston shook his head slowly. He looked as though he was on the verge of tears.

The reporter turned once again to face the camera. "So John *something*, the fire warden on the eighty-fifth floor, is one of the hundreds of unknown heroes who saved lives. This is one of the themes we have heard continually–people risking their lives to save others, putting the lives of total strangers above their own safety. So, John, if you're out there and you hear this report, would you please call in? We all want to hear from you. We *all* want to know that you made it out. Now back to our main desk."

The scene shifted to two anchormen sitting behind a big desk. My father had found the remote, and he muted the sound.

"Are you going to call?" my mother asked.

He gave her a questioning look.

"You should at least let them know your name."

"Nobody needs to know my name."

"Don't you think Dennis Johnston would like to know your name, would like to know you're alive? Wouldn't that be reassuring, comforting for him?" my mother said.

"I guess you're right. I'll call when I have time, later today."

"Do you want me to call for you?" my mother asked.

"I'd appreciate that."

The scene on the TV shifted to the site of the World Trade Center, or what was left of it.

"Wow," I gasped. "It's just so hard to believe."

"It is," my father agreed. "It's like a war zone."

The scene was of twisted metal, a few columns still standing, and the latticework facing of one of the buildings standing ten stories high. But most of what the Twin Towers had been was flattened to the ground in a gigantic pile that seemed to go on forever. Smoke was rising from a dozen spots across the rubble, and the whole area seemed to be in a fog or mist. Obviously there were still fires burning beneath the surface.

I tried to picture where we'd been when the first tower had fallen, but I didn't think we had the right angle, or maybe it had all been covered with debris when the second tower fell.

Surrounding the debris from the fallen towers were those buildings that were still standing, barely. They had gaping holes, entire sides ripped open, crumpled floors, and they had the strange appearance of having almost melted . . . dripping down, distorted, angles all wrong, like they were made of plastic that had been left too close to a fire.

Moving throughout the pile, like little ants, were people. Some were obviously police or firefighters, all in uniform, but others wore construction helmets and were removing the rubble. They were all probably searching for survivors. But looking at the scene, like that, I wondered how anybody could have survived.

"And we walked right through it," I said out loud.

"We were so close that we couldn't really see it. At least not like this," my father said.

"And on the TV was the only way I could see it," my mother said. "Just staring at the set, not knowing if you were alive or . . ."

She started to cry again, and both my father and I put our arms around her.

"I . . . I was so helpless . . . And I called and called, but I couldn't get through to you on your cellphone . . ."

"All the cell towers were overwhelmed with people trying to make calls," my father explained. "And the stairwells were dead reception zones, I think."

"I was just calling and calling," she sobbed. "And then when the building collapsed and I still couldn't get you . . ." She started to shake and sob even louder.

My mother was what my father called "a worrier." She always worried when my father was late and hadn't called us, so he always tried to call. With me, it was even worse. She always wanted to know exactly where I was and who I was with. And, of course, being a teenager, I was always trying to be sure she *didn't* know where I was or who I was with. Generally, though, I did let her know at least a version of the truth. That just made life easier for everybody.

"The important thing is that we're all right," my father said. "We're right here."

"But you could have been killed," she sobbed.

"But we weren't."

"I know . . . I know . . . Thank God. I just stared at the TV and prayed."

"I'm just glad you didn't have to go through it alone," my father said.

My aunt—my mother's sister—and some of the neighbors had been with her. They'd still been here when we'd finally got home, just before eleven. We were greeted with cheers and tears, practically mobbed. Some of these people had been our neighbors for years, but I'd never even talked to them except to maybe say hello, or we'd wave at each other when we drove past. Strange how, suddenly, they were acting like family.

"You know, I think it was harder watching than it would have been to have actually been there," my mother said.

My eyes opened wide in shock and met my father's gaze. He shrugged, and his eyes pleaded with me not to say anything. After what we'd gone through, how could she even *think* that it had been worse for her?

"I know that sounds awful . . . insensitive," my mother said. "But I would rather have been there with you two, knowing that you were alive, than been here without you."

That opened my eyes again. I *did* understand. At least we knew.

"We called as soon as we could," my father said. "We just couldn't call right away."

We'd left the building just before it collapsed. We were showered with debris, knocked off our feet, and practically suffocated in the cloud of dust that overwhelmed everything and blotted out the sun. That was maybe the scariest part of the whole day. Scary because I'd thought we were finally safe. Scary because my father wasn't with me at the very moment the tower collapsed, and for a few short seconds—half a minute maybe—I'd thought he was dead. Maybe I could understand what my mother had gone through. And for her it wasn't a few short seconds. It was hours.

"It's the president," my mother said, pointing at the TV set.

President Bush was sitting at his desk in the Oval Office, looking solemn but calm. Underneath was a caption indicating that this was a rebroadcast of a speech he'd given yesterday. My father hit the Mute button again so we could hear him speak.

"Good evening. Today, our fellow citizens, our way of life, our very freedom came under attack in a series of deliberate and deadly terrorist acts. The victims were in airplanes, or in their offices; secretaries, businessmen and -women, military and federal workers; moms and dads, friends and neighbors. Thousands of lives were suddenly ended by evil, despicable acts of terror."

Down below, on the banner that ran across the screen, it said that the main suspect in the attacks was someone named Osama bin Laden, leader of a terrorist group in Afghanistan. That was hard to get my head around—what gripe did Afghanistan have with America? My dad had talked about religious extremists when we were trying to get out, trying to make some sense of what had happened. Was that who these guys were? And then came the updated numbers: "Death toll believed to exceed 3,000, with injuries to over 7,000."

That seven thousand included me and my father.

"These acts of mass murder were intended to frighten our nation into chaos and retreat. But they have failed; our country is strong.

"A great people has been moved to defend a great nation. Terrorist attacks can shake the foundation of our biggest buildings, but they cannot touch the foundation of America. These acts shattered steel, but they cannot dent the steel of American resolve."

I felt a chill go up my spine. The president—*my* president—was speaking out for all of us, speaking about something that had happened to me.

"Today, our nation saw evil, the very worst of human nature. And we responded with the best of America—with the daring of our rescue workers, with the caring for strangers and neighbors who came to give blood and help in any way they could."

I knew what my father had done, what we'd *both* done. And I thought about all the policemen and firefighters . . . Oh my God, I'd forgotten about James's father. He'd been one of the firemen going up while we'd been going down. I didn't know what had happened to him. I had to call James. What sort of a friend was I—what sort of *best* friend—to have forgotten about him? No, calling him on the phone wasn't enough. I had to go over to his house. Immediately, right now. I started to speak but stopped myself. I couldn't interrupt the president.

"This is a day when all Americans from every walk of life unite in our resolve for justice and peace. America has stood down enemies before, and we will do so this time. None of us

*will ever forget this day. Yet, we go forward to defend freedom
and all that is good and just in our world.*

"Thank you. Good night and God bless America."

The president's image faded and it was back to the news anchors. My father muted the sound again.

"The president spoke for all of us," my father said. "Strange, this is one of the darkest events in our history, but I know we're going to rise above it. I have no doubts."

"I just can't stop thinking about the people who aren't going to rise above it," I said. "The three thousand people who died."

"And their families," my mother added.

"I need to go and see James and his family," I said.

"I already called, and we might go to see them tonight," my mother said.

"No, I need to see James before that . . . Wait, you were talking to them?" I asked.

"I called and spoke to James's mother this morning."

"And have they heard anything?" I asked, although I was almost afraid to get the answer.

She shook her head. "They're still waiting. Sometimes the waiting is the hardest part."

"I have to go over there right now."

"You need to come into the kitchen, sit down, and eat breakfast. Both of you."

"I'm not hungry," I said.

"And I'd better continue to try to make arrangements for—"

"No," my mother said forcefully, cutting my father

off. "Both of you have been through a lot, physically and mentally, and you need to eat. Right after breakfast you can get back on the phone, John, and I'll take Will over to see the Bennetts."

"I can walk over," I said.

"I know you can, but I want to go as well."

"I'm okay, you don't have to be right there with me."

"I'm not going for you. I'm going for James's mother. I think I know what she's going through as much as anybody else can. Now, breakfast first."

CHAPTER
TWO

My mother shoveled another pile of scrambled eggs onto our plates—my third helping, Dad's second. I did want to get over to James's house, but I was still hungry. It was like the food was filling a gigantic empty pit in my stomach. That really shouldn't have been a surprise. Before we'd left for my father's office yesterday I'd been too rushed to eat much breakfast, and then, with everything that happened, there was no chance to eat—not that I was thinking about food then. Somehow the strange combination of danger and adrenaline I'd been dining on had suppressed not only my appetite but even the thought that I needed to eat. It was as if my stomach had closed down the same time my brain and muscles kicked into gear. Finally, at the mobile hospital where they were stitching me up, I ate a muffin—one stale muffin. Then, when I did get home, instead of eating I just fell into bed and passed out, exhausted, spent, numb.

Funny, though I was eating now but I really couldn't even taste the food. It was like when you have a really bad cold and all your food tastes bland, except now it just didn't taste like anything at all.

"It's so good to see you both eating," my mother said.

"The food is great," my father said.

"It is great," I agreed. I wasn't going to tell her I couldn't taste it. With my mother it was like, *Love me, love my food.*

Both my father and I had coughing fits during the meal. My mother warned us to "stop wolfing down" the food, but we knew what was really going on. There was just no point in talking about it and scaring her. She refilled my glass with orange juice. I'd already drained the glass three times. I wasn't really thirsty; it was more the way it felt going down. My throat was raw and sore. Who knew what was in that air that we'd had to breathe when the building collapsed? Was that why I couldn't taste anything? Maybe it was best for now that I didn't think about it.

The doorbell rang and I started to get up to answer it, but my mother put a hand on my shoulder to keep me in my seat.

"You eat, I'll get it." She left the kitchen and went to the door.

"She's just worried about us," my father said quietly.

"Yeah, but there's nothing to worry about now."

"I don't know. I'm worried about you."

"Me? I'm here and I'm fine. A little cut up, but these are nothing," I said, holding up my hands.

"That's not what I'm talking about, Will. We almost died yesterday. We saw people die—you saw people choose to jump from the tower rather than die in the flames. There's no way something like that doesn't have an impact." He leaned across the table and gently took both of my hands in his. "But we're going to get through this. I'm going to help you, and you're going to help me. We'll get through this the same way we got through yesterday. Together."

"Together."

My mother walked back into the kitchen, smiling. "Your guest has arrived." Suzie was right behind her.

My father got to his feet and gave her a big hug. She was so little and he was so big that she practically disappeared into his arms.

"You're next," she said to me.

I felt uneasy, but she came over and gave me a big hug as well. She started to cry. There was a lot of that going on.

"No time for tears," she said as she brushed them from her face. "We have to get down to business."

"No, you have to sit down and have some coffee, and maybe a bagel," my mother said.

"But we have—"

"Don't even try to argue with my wife," my father said. He pulled out a chair for Suzie.

"Tell me . . . tell us what happened to you after we last saw you," my father said.

"You know what happened," she said.

"I want to know what happened to *you*, how you got out."

She shrugged. "I walked down the stairs."

"I know. How far did you get before the plane hit?" my father asked.

"Pretty far. Maybe around the sixtieth floor."

"That's good. You were well below the crash floors."

"It didn't feel like that. The whole building shook. It felt like it was right overtop of us. And that's when everything changed."

"Changed how?" I asked.

"There were people on the stairs before, but after that it just became a flood of people. It wasn't like they were pushing or shoving, but they were scared. Everybody wanted to hurry now, but because of the crowd we had to move slower."

"Did you go down with anybody else from the office?"

She shook her head. "I started down last, remember?"

Suzie had wanted to stay with us, and it was only after my father had pushed her into the stairwell that she'd joined the others already on their way down.

"Then everybody else should have been on a lower floor than you," my father said.

"Everybody except you two. About the twentieth floor I saw the first firefighters going up. I asked them what had happened . . . where it had happened. And when they told me, I just prayed that you two had made it below the floor where it hit in time."

"I wish we had," my father said. "So, you didn't see anybody else from the office at any time?"

"I ran into Jenna in the concourse. We talked for a while and she left. I wanted to stay there to wait for you two, but the police wouldn't let me—they just sort of whisked me away."

"So, where were you when the building collapsed?" my father asked.

"I was on Broadway, four or five blocks north. From where I was I didn't even see the building go down. I heard the sound, but my view was blocked by another building, and then I saw the smoke, the cloud . . . people started running and screaming . . . I started running, but it stopped. It never got as far as me." She paused. "And then I heard what had happened. I couldn't believe it. How could that tower fall? And once I knew it was true, all I could think of was that you two were still up there." She turned to my mother. "When you called me last night to tell me they were okay . . . you have no idea how incredible that call was. That was one of the best telephone calls I ever received in my whole life."

"I think I have some idea," my mother said.

"Oh, of course. What am I thinking?" Suzie apologized.

"That's okay. I wasn't trying to make you feel bad. I was just glad I could let you know. I made a lot of happy phone calls between the time the boys called me and the time they arrived home."

"So, what about your story?" Suzie asked.

"It's like yours. We went down the stairs," my father said, and shrugged.

"What floor were you on when the plane hit?" Suzie asked.

"We were still—"

"In all the confusion it's hard to say exactly," my father said, cutting me off.

My mother and Suzie exchanged a look. I didn't think either of them believed him.

"I know you're just trying to protect me," my mother said. "But it's important that I know what you went through . . . the whole thing."

"Okay, all right . . . I know you're right. We were . . . we were still on our floor."

"You were still on eighty-five?" Suzie sounded amazed, shocked.

"But that's *above* the floors where the plane hit!" My mother was definitely alarmed.

My father slowly nodded his head.

"But . . . but . . . why didn't you tell me?"

"It just . . . didn't come up," my father said.

My father and I had made an agreement not to tell her everything right away—not that we were going to lie to her, but we were going to sort of "withhold" some of the information. Now the cat was pretty much out of the bag.

"I wish I'd known," she said. "Is there anything else you haven't mentioned?"

"No, nothing."

I nodded my head in agreement, and she looked a little bit relieved.

"It's better that I know."

"I want to know too. How did you get down?" Suzie asked.

"Like I said, we went down the stairs," my father answered.

"It couldn't have been that easy," Suzie said.

Before my father could downplay it again I jumped in. "It wasn't that easy. There was smoke, and people said the stairwells were all blocked. A man said there was no way down and we should go up, but Dad said we had to try to get down."

"I knew we could always go up later, but we had to at least try going down first," my father said.

"And you got past those floors where the fire was?"

"Yes."

"How? What was it like?" Suzie asked.

I didn't know what to say. How could any of it be put into words? It looked like my father was having the same problem because he didn't answer either.

"I understand if you don't want to talk about it," my mother said.

"No," my father said, shaking his head, "it's just that I'm looking for the words." I wasn't sure if he didn't know what to say, or if he *knew* but was searching for the right way to put it so my mother wouldn't be even more upset.

"It was . . . There were . . . flames . . . and smoke . . . heat . . . and the smell . . . It was just like . . . like . . ."

"Like hell," I said, my voice barely a whisper.

My father looked over at me and nodded. "Like Hell. I always thought hell was somewhere down below, but it was up there in the sky, and we walked right by it, passed right through it."

"I wanted to go up," I said. "I thought we should go up."

"That was just for a few seconds," my father said. "You were with me all the way. You were brave all the way."

I wanted to say something about how that wasn't true, but I kept silent.

"Without our son I wouldn't have made it," he said to my mother. "It was because of him that I made the decision to go down."

"You would have done that even if I hadn't been there," I said.

"I don't think so. But even so, there was no way I would have made it down in time without you. Think about Ting."

"Ting? Did you say Ting?" my mother asked.

I looked at my father. I'd gone to sleep almost as soon as we got home. Obviously he hadn't told her about Ting, either.

"There was a message this morning, before you got up." My mother went to the counter and started sifting through a pile of message notes. "There were so many calls . . . so many people wanting to speak to me or to you or—"

"Did Ting call?" my father asked.

"I think so . . . maybe . . . but I had trouble understanding her . . . I didn't really understand what she was saying because she didn't speak English very—"

"Ting doesn't speak much English," I said. "But how did she get our number?" I asked my father.

"I gave it to her when we left her to be taken to the hospital. I just didn't think she'd call so soon."

"Here it is." My mother handed a little yellow slip to my father. I could see a number and name on the paper. Ting had left her number.

"Who exactly is Ting?" Suzie asked.

"We met her on the way down the stairs," my father explained.

"We *carried* her down the stairs," I said.

"You did what?" my mother asked.

"We found her on one of the floors," my father said.

"The *seventy-fourth* floor," I added.

"She was hurt. We carried her down on our backs."

"Down seventy-four floors?" Suzie asked.

"She wasn't big," my father said. "She couldn't have weighed any more than a hundred pounds, wouldn't you say, Will?"

"Not much more. She didn't weigh much at all."

"And we took turns," my father said. "It wasn't like I did it by myself. I *couldn't* have done it by myself. Not without resting every few floors. If Will hadn't been with me then neither Ting nor I would have made it out in time." He turned directly to me. "That's what I mean about your saving *my* life."

"I just can't believe that you carried somebody down seventy-four floors," my mother said.

"*We* carried her down," my father said. "Besides, can you believe that we'd leave an injured person behind?"

"No," both Suzie and my mother said at the same time.

"Her leg was hurt," I said. "That's why we had to carry her."

"I was more worried about the head injury," my father added. "I'm glad she called. That must mean she's feeling okay. Maybe I should call her back."

"After you finish the story," Suzie said.

"I think we have finished. We got out of the tower, it fell down, and we got home."

I could tell my father was trying to minimize things and not let anybody know how close we came to not getting out.

"Where were you when it collapsed?" my mother asked. She wasn't going to let him off again, and he knew it. She'd figured out what he was doing.

"We were there. Right there," he said. "I was one of the last people who got out. When the building came down the force of the air rushing away just picked me up and tossed me like a rag doll."

My mother gasped.

"But Will was farther away."

"It knocked me over, and I was hit with all sorts

of stuff . . . Now I know what it's like to be a sock in a dryer."

"A sock in a dryer with a handful of nails, a drawerful of knives, and a couple of doorknobs thrown in for good measure," my father added.

"That's where you got all the cuts and bruises," my mother said.

I nodded. "We were lucky that's all we got. The way everything was flying around we could have gotten . . ." I stopped myself. "But mostly the problem was with the dust."

"You were *in* that cloud that I ran from?" Suzie asked.

"Right in the middle. It blocked out the sun, and it felt like there was no air. It was like breathing sand, like I was being suffocated."

"I heard on the news that most of the concrete from the floors was pulverized into that dust," Suzie said.

"Not all of it," I said. "There were chunks falling all around us."

"Maybe that dust explains why the two of you are coughing so much," my mother said. "I want you to go and see Dr. Tamari. I want him to do a full physical on both of you."

"We were seen yesterday when they stitched us up," my father said. "Besides, Dr. Tamari is probably overwhelmed today. Let's give it a day or so."

"Okay, a day or so, but I'm calling to set up appointments for you two for later this week and we're not going to have any arguments, understand?"

We weren't going to disagree. I knew there was no point. Besides, I thought seeing a doctor wouldn't be the worst thing in the world. I was really okay, but I did want to stop coughing.

"First things first," my father said. "Suzie and I need to make some phone calls."

"And I need to go and see James."

"I'll drive you over."

"Thanks. I'll get ready."

I knew I could wash up. I knew I could get clean clothes on. But I didn't know if I was going to be *ready*. I had no idea what I was going to say when I got there.

CHAPTER
THREE

My mother slowed the car down as we pulled up to James's house. There was no space in the driveway—there were already four cars there—and there were tons of cars parked on the street. School had been cancelled and most businesses had shut down for the day, so nobody had gone to work. It looked as though there were people there already at the Bennetts'. Maybe a lot of people. I wondered if that would make it easier. Or harder. What did I know?

We pulled into a spot in front of a house a bit farther down the street. My mother turned off the engine, and we both sat there. Neither of us made any move to get out. It was like we thought if we didn't get out of the car we wouldn't have to go into the house and face whatever was happening there.

"We can sit here as long as you want," my mother said. It was like she was reading my mind.

"Thanks. I just need a few minutes. I'm not sure what to say to anybody."

"Sometimes it isn't necessary to say anything. Just being there is comforting," she told me.

"Really?"

My mother nodded. "It made me feel better to have people with me yesterday . . . when I didn't know about . . . about what had happened to you and your father."

She looked as though she was going to start crying again.

"Let's go in, then. I need to see James. I just wish we could have picked him up and taken him home yesterday like we promised his father."

"You tried."

James had gone to work with his father that day, like I'd gone with mine, as part of this "take your kid to work" thing they wanted us to do at school. When the plane hit, the call came in for his father's fire crew—every crew in the whole city—to respond to the emergency at the World Trade Center, and James had to stay behind at the station.

We'd found that out on the way down the stairs. There, in the middle of everything—us heading down, carrying Ting, and firefighters heading up, loaded down with equipment, looking for people to help—we ran into Mr. Bennett. It was one of the most strange, bizarre moments in a day full of strange, bizarre moments. We stopped for just a minute—less than a minute—and he asked us if we could drop by his station and get James and take him home. We promised we would, and then he hurried up the stairs, back toward the danger, and we started back down. I remembered watching him as he caught up with the other firefighters. I saw one last little glimpse of him as he turned the corner and was gone. Other than his crew, we must have been the last people to talk to him. Not his wife or his kids. Us. Me and my father, there in the stairwell.

If I'd only known, I would have asked him what he wanted us to say to his family, or . . . That was stupid. If I'd known what was going to happen, that the whole tower was going to fall, I would have told him and he would have come down with us. Wouldn't he?

After we got out of the tower and away from the collapse the first thing we did was get medical treatment. But right after that we tried to call the fire station to talk to James, to tell him we were coming to get him. We couldn't get through at first. And then when we did finally get a line we were told that the department had arranged a drive home for James and he wasn't there any more.

At first I was grateful. I was exhausted, and I just wanted to get home myself as fast as possible. That was part of it. But there was more. I didn't know what

I was supposed to say to him. Was I supposed to be the one to tell him that his father had probably been in the tower when it collapsed? That I didn't see any way he could have survived?

Now, a day later, I still didn't know what to say. At least I didn't have to tell him what had happened, because by now he already knew.

Maybe my mother was right and I didn't really have to say anything. Maybe just being there would be enough. Either way, I'd soon find out.

"Okay, let's just go," I said.

We lived outside the city—a thirty-minute train ride from my father's office . . . where his office used to be. There were sort of two sections to the neighborhood, one with big houses and the other with houses that were . . . were . . . less big. James lived in the second section. Not that the houses weren't nice. They were almost all neat and well cared for, but they were much smaller than ours—tidy little bungalows and houses that had had second stories built on. The people who lived here were teachers, nurses, tradespeople, and police and firefighters. I wondered how many more people on this street were waiting for a call they hoped wouldn't come.

We walked up the front path. The grass was cut and the flower beds well tended. James's father liked doing yard work. He used an old push mower. He'd told me once that it just made the grass look better, that the push-mower blades didn't "bruise" the grass. I could just picture him out there, working, waving to me as I walked up, a big smile on his face, earbuds from his iPod in his ears, listening to music—old school Zeppelin, Stones, and AC/DC. Even if I couldn't hear the music I could often hear him singing along as he worked.

He was always so friendly, happy. All the guys liked him. He would come out to toss a ball with us or play road hockey or shoot some hoops. Sometimes when a bunch of us were down in the basement he'd just order a pizza for us, bring it down, and hand it over—of course, minus the two pieces that he'd eaten.

Just the day before yesterday he'd come down when we were jamming in the basement, picked up an old guitar, and started playing along. He was pretty good—mostly old school, but he knew his stuff.

It wasn't unusual for him to be around the house, which made him really different from most of our dads. Firefighters lived at the station house for a bunch of days in a row and then got days off, so he seemed to be home a lot. It would make it that much stranger for him to not be around any more. Somehow it didn't seem possible that he wouldn't be there. I had to stop thinking that way—I shouldn't just be writing him off in my mind. That wasn't

right.

Coming up to the front door seemed strange. I usually went around the side and in through the kitchen door. It was never locked. I'd just walk into the house, yell out a hello, and head either into the basement or up to James's room.

My mother pressed the doorbell. There was no turning back now. I heard somebody coming to the door. Would it be James or his mother or . . . ? The door opened. It was some strange, older woman I didn't know.

"Hello," my mother said. "We're here to see Becky and James."

"Becky's not really accepting visitors right now," the woman said.

"I think . . . I think she'd want to see us. Could you just tell her that it's Samantha and Will Fuller . . . please?"

She nodded. "I'll ask her. Please wait." She closed the door, leaving us standing on the front stoop. I was stunned. My mother looked surprised as well.

"I guess they want to make sure that the family isn't being bothered by people who just—"

The door swung open, interrupting my mother. It was Mrs. Bennett!

"I'm so sorry!" she exclaimed. She gave us a big smile. She was happy to see us, and I was already glad that we'd come. "Please, please come in . . . I'm so sorry . . . my aunt is just trying to protect us. She didn't know who you were!"

"We understand completely," my mother said.

She ushered us in and gave both of us a hug. She looked at me, hard, surveying me up and down. "Were you injured?" she asked.

"No, not really. Just my hands, a little."

She reached out and took my hands to examine them. "That looks painful," she said, referring to the stitches.

"It's nothing, really; it doesn't even hurt."

"I'm sure it does, but you're being brave." She let go of my hands and looked at my mother. "And your husband?"

"He got it a little worse. Three fractured ribs, a concussion, and a separated elbow."

"Sam has had the first two, but not the third. Men can be such babies when they're hurt or sick."

"Isn't that the truth," my mother agreed.

I guess I was being insulted, but what could I say?

"Will, James is going to be so happy to see you. You know how it is when you're surrounded all day by nothing but a bunch of silly adults."

"Yeah, I guess."

"Normally he'd at least have his father around, and that's like having another kid," she said. "But you'd know that."

I'd heard her say that more than once, but really, he was like a big kid. He never seemed to be worried about things like my father was. I'd never even seen him in a suit and tie.

"Please come into the kitchen. I just put on a fresh pot of coffee and I baked some muffins. And, of course, people have brought food."

There were a dozen people in the kitchen already. Some older women—like her aunt—a couple of men, a neighbor I recognized, and James's little sister, Amanda. But there was no James.

We were greeted with a few quiet words and solemn nods. Many of these people looked as though they'd been crying. They looked distraught, upset, and scared all rolled into one. The only one who didn't look sad was Mrs. Bennett. She didn't look—or act—the way I'd thought she would. She was smiling and her voice was all cheery, and if she'd been crying she'd fixed her makeup so well that you couldn't tell.

"Have you heard anything?" my mother asked.

That was so like my mother, straight to the point, fearless.

"They're all pretty busy today, but the department has been keeping us updated," she said. "And, of course, we have CNN."

There was a small television on in the corner. The sound was so low that I could barely hear it, but there were a couple of men sitting right in front of it, watching intently. Right now on the screen there was footage of something that looked like some kind of military camp, where guys were getting weapons training. The voiceover was saying something about terrorist groups in Afghanistan and one in particular called Al Qaeda. Were these amateurs the guys responsible for all this devastation? It was hard to believe.

"I expect we'll get good news soon," she said sweetly.

Good news? What good news did she expect to hear? My father had told her what happened when he'd called last night to make sure James was home safe. It was the last thing I remembered hearing before I dropped into a deep stupor. He'd told her that we'd seen her husband going up the stairs as we were going down, so she had to figure that he was in the building when it collapsed. I mean, we'd barely made it out and we were going the right way. He couldn't possibly have survived . . . could he?

"The department says there are reports coming in all the time," she continued. "They pulled three people out of the wreckage today already and—"

"They just found another person," one of the men at the TV said. "They just announced it."

"That's so wonderful!" Mrs. Bennett said. "That's another husband going home to his wife, another father going home to his children. I expect *my* husband to walk in that door any minute." Her smile faltered for just a brief second and then came back to full glow. "At least he'll call me."

One of the women went up and put her arm around her. "I'm sure he'll call. I'm sure."

"Thanks. Now, Will, you came here to see James. He's downstairs in the rec room. You *certainly* know the way."

"Yeah . . . sure . . . thanks."

I was grateful for an excuse to leave the room. I couldn't understand what was going on. It was like Mrs. Bennett just didn't understand. It was like she was playing a game or pretending.

Before I hit the bottom of the stairs I heard a guitar being played—it was James. I'd jammed with him enough to know what his licks sounded like. I stopped and listened.

I knew the song. It was something that he and I had written together. It was a really cool riff that we were still working on, although it did sound like he'd worked out a few more chords. But why was he working on the song? Was he downstairs doing with the guitar what his mother was upstairs doing with the muffins? Was he just pretending that none of this had happened, that his father wasn't dead? How could he not be dead? How could he have survived that collapse? I'd come here thinking I was going to have to deal with people crying or screaming, but instead it was almost like nothing was wrong. No, they had to know. They weren't stupid people.

I stood there frozen on the stairs. I had to fight the urge to spin around and go back up. I couldn't do that. Actually I didn't want to be there, either. I was stuck between two places I didn't want to be. I guess it was easier to just let gravity make the decision.

I went down the last few steps and into the rec room. James was sitting in the corner, on a stool, playing his guitar. He looked up. He gave me a slight nod, a slight smile, to acknowledge my being there, but continued to play, continued to focus on the song. I walked over and perched on the arm of the couch and watched.

He finished the riff. "What do you think?" he asked.

"Not bad. Might work good. Wait."

I walked over and picked up my bass. I slung it around my neck, adjusted the strap, and plugged it into the amp. James started to play, and I started along the bass line. We'd played this part a hundred times before and it *did* sound good to me. It could have been that I liked it because we'd written it, or simply that we'd played it so much that it was like one of those McDonald's commercials that you hear so often it just lodges in your brain against your will until you're humming it and it's driving you crazy and—no, it really *was* good.

We came up to the new part, the part he'd written, and as James started off I tried to follow on the bass. I plucked a few notes. I thought I had it! This could really work and— James stopped playing.

"That wasn't right," he said.

"It's my first time through," I apologized. "I can get it better once I've heard it a couple more times."

He unplugged his guitar and lifted it by the strap until he was holding it over his head.

"Not the song," he said. His voice was barely above a whisper.

He was frozen now, staring straight ahead, his expression a complete blank, like a mask that I couldn't read. I looked at him silently staring. Was I supposed to say something, or was I supposed to just wait until he said something?

James suddenly unfroze. He jumped to his feet, grabbed his guitar by the neck, and smashed it against the wall! I jumped up and almost toppled over in shock, but before I could do or say anything, he swung the guitar against the wall again and again and again, until the neck snapped and all that was holding the two pieces together were the strings.

There was a noise at the top of the stairs. "Are you all right down there?" It was a male voice, but I didn't recognize it.

I looked at James. He didn't answer. Things were far from okay, but what was I supposed to say?

"James!" the voice called out louder. "Is anything wrong?"

"Nothing!" he called back. "Nothing is wrong."

There was a pause. "We heard something," the voice said.

"It was just my guitar."

That certainly wasn't a lie.

"It's all right," James said. "Don't worry . . . don't worry."

He slumped back down on the stool. I heard the upstairs door close. I stood there, still in shock, looking at James holding his broken guitar—a guitar he loved more than he loved his girlfriend—wondering what I was supposed to say.

Slowly I took off my bass and set it down. For a quick, terrible second, I thought about how I should take my bass with me when I left, in case he smashed it, too, but then I put that thought away. He wouldn't hurt my bass. And if he did, well, that would be what he needed to do, and I guess I'd have to understand.

I walked over until I was standing right in front of him. He looked up from the guitar to me. His expression was sad and sorry and confused. It was almost as if, even though he was looking down at the broken guitar, he didn't know how it had got that way. More likely he was searching for what to say to explain what he'd done, and hoping I'd give him those words.

Gently I took the guitar from him. I put it down on the couch, laying the two pieces together so it still looked like a guitar.

"It's just a guitar," I said. "It can be fixed."

"It *can't* be fixed," he said.

"I don't know. Maybe some guitar guy can use glue or—"

"I'm not talking about the guitar."

I suddenly knew what he meant.

"No matter how many muffins you bake, no matter how much you smile, no matter how hard you pray or how much you wish, it can't be fixed."

"I know," I mumbled.

"Do you?"

"I think I do . . . I think I understand."

"Then could you go upstairs and explain it to my mother?" he asked. "She has to know . . . has to know the truth." He started to sob and shake. I put an arm around his shoulders. What else could I do?

"I just feel so guilty," James sobbed.

"Guilty of what?" I sputtered. What did he mean by that?

"I should have been there. I should have gone with him."

"You know you couldn't have," I said. "You told me that they weren't going to let you go on any calls, that they wouldn't let you go with them in the truck for anything."

"I should have gone anyway. I should have just gone and walked there once I knew what was going on, once I saw it on TV. I should have walked. The station is just a few blocks away . . . I could have gone there to find him."

"You couldn't have found him," I said. "It was just crazy . . . confused . . . You couldn't have found him."

"Maybe I could have," James said.

"Even if you did find him, what difference would it have made?" I asked. "He had his job to do."

"I could have just gone into the building and—"

"And done what?"

"I could have been with him."

"And died too?"

He stopped crying and looked up at me, square into my eyes. I knew what I'd just said, and I knew he'd heard it— *"and died too"* —that's what I'd said.

"He is dead, isn't he?" he said, his voice catching on each word.

Of course he was dead. There really couldn't be any question about that, could there? But who was I to say?

I shrugged. "I don't know. I don't know anything." Maybe that wasn't honest, but in a way it was the truth. Really, I didn't know. Not for sure.

"Boys!" a voice called out loudly from upstairs. "They've found some people alive in the wreckage . . . some firefighters!"

CHAPTER
FOUR

James and I flew up the steps, pounding the stairs as we ran, racing into the kitchen. Everybody was crowded around the little TV and the volume was up as high as it could go. People made way for James to squeeze through to the front, where his mother and sister were already standing. I stopped at the back and shifted so I could see past the heads in front of me to the picture.

Two anchorpeople were sitting at their desk.

"Yes, we have reports of a rescue of seven people—I repeat, seven people—from the wreckage," the female anchor said.

"And these are confirmed reports," the male anchor added.

"Yes, confirmed. We have had many reports of people being pulled out of the wreckage, but most often these have proven to be unfounded."

"I have been told that the seven people include five members of New York's bravest, our firefighters."

You could almost feel the mood in the kitchen change. Everybody stayed silent, but there were smiles, or hints of smiles. I tried to see the expression on James's face or his mother's or even his sister's, but I could see only the backs of their heads.

"We're going to go live to Ground Zero for a report shortly," the woman said. "But at this time we can confirm that seven people, including a Port Authority police officer and five firefighters, have been pulled from the wreckage." Her voice caught over the last few words and I thought she was about to cry.

Along the bottom of the screen on the crawl it was repeating what they had just said. Somehow that made it all more real, because I wasn't just hearing it, I was reading it.

"We're going to go live now, down to the site, where our reporter has Chief Donovan standing by."

The scene changed to two men, one obviously the chief and the other a reporter. The chief's face was dirty, and he looked as though he hadn't slept. Behind them was the wreckage, filtered through a film of smoke—or was it mist, or steam, or dust?

"Chief, can you update us on the story of more survivors being found?"

"I'm happy to report that we've located seven more survivors. I can now confirm that one of them is a Port Authority police officer and five are firefighters."

A little burst of excitement filled the kitchen. People reached over and patted others, or gave them a squeeze, and those hints of smiles became fully blown. I started to cough and turned away, covering my mouth to try to muffle the sound.

"And can you tell me the condition of those survivors?"

"They report only minor injuries."

This time a cheer went up in the room.

"But they haven't been examined by medical personnel," the chief said. "In fact, they haven't yet been fully extricated from the wreckage."

"So they remain trapped."

"It's not so much that they're trapped as that we are taking great care to make sure they are removed safely."

"Can you give us the circumstances of their situation?"

"They are trapped in the remains of a stairwell."

"Stairwell," I said out loud. "That's where—"

"That's where my husband was last seen," Mrs. Bennett said. She turned around, scanning the room. "Will?"

I started slightly. She was calling me. I moved slightly so she could see me, so she was looking right at me.

"Will, that's where my husband was when you saw him . . . He was in the stairwell . . . right?"

"Yes, in the stairwell."

She smiled and nodded her head.

But weren't most of the firefighters in stairwells? I thought but didn't say. They were all heading up the stairs to get to the people who were trapped. They were heading up to try to fight the fires on the top floors. That's why they were carrying all the equipment—putting out the fires would have allowed the people on the top ten floors to be rescued.

"You said there were seven people," the reporter questioned.

"The seventh person is apparently a woman who was being assisted in her evacuation by the firefighters."

"Can you tell us her name, and the names of the firefighters?"

The room became hushed. I felt another cough coming up but worked hard to suppress it.

"We know the names, but we are not prepared to release them until these people are fully free from the wreckage."

"And how long do you estimate that will take?" the reporter asked.

"There are no estimates of the—"

"Wait," the reporter said, holding a hand up to his ear. He must have been wearing an earpiece. "I'm receiving word that the rescue has begun, that the first person is being removed."

The camera showed a woman—an older black woman—being walked, a paramedic on each side. Her clothes were ripped and torn, her face caked with white powder, and she had a bandage wrapped around her head. She smiled and gave a little wave, and a cheer went up in the background. They lowered her onto a waiting stretcher.

"That is Josephine Harris," the unseen announcer said. "Reports indicate that the firefighters trapped in the stairwell with her were helping her to leave the building at the time of the evacuation. Due to health issues or possibly injuries she was not able to move rapidly, and they were unwilling to leave her behind."

"A firefighter would never leave a civilian behind," Mrs. Bennett said to a round of nodding heads and supportive comments.

"And here are the first of the firefighters," the announcer said.

Two firefighters, again assisted by paramedics, walked toward the camera. Their heads were down, their faces filthy, clothing ripping, helmets missing—but one of them had a mustache and was the right size, and there was something about the way he walked . . . Was it possible that . . . ? He looked up at the camera. It wasn't him. I looked again, harder, trying to convince myself, but it definitely wasn't Mr. Bennett.

I felt my whole body—physically and emotionally— sag.

The two men were helped to waiting stretchers.

On the screen another man was loaded onto a stretcher. We couldn't see his face, but as he was being carried he lifted his arm and gave a thumbs-up to the crowd, and there was more cheering.

"Injuries of the rescued are reported to include burns, concussions, a separated shoulder, and broken bones, but nothing life-threatening," the announcer reported. "And we take you now to a press conference, where they are going to release the names of those who have just been rescued from the wreckage of the World Trade Center collapse."

Four men in firefighters' uniforms, probably chiefs, stood behind a podium. In front of them were dozens and dozens of men and women, reporters, with microphones and cameras, all jostling forward to hear what was about to be said.

"On a day of tragedy," one of the fire chiefs began, "we are thrilled to report that we have found seven more survivors, and that five of them are members of our family."

His face lightened, and it looked as if he was fighting back tears.

"The rescue workers were in the process of evacuating the building and were down to the fourth floor when the tower collapsed," the announcer said. "They reported that they were thrown down the stairs, hit by falling debris, and trapped in the stairwell, which somehow remained intact."

"Just tell us their names," one of the men over from me said, speaking what we were all thinking.

"The men were rescued from stairwell B of the North Tower," the fire chief said.

North Tower? But Mr. Bennett was in the South Tower. That's where we'd seen him, that's where my father's office was. That was the staircase we were going down when we saw him going up. This couldn't be him.

I looked at my mother. Her expression mirrored my thoughts, but nobody else was reacting. They didn't know that it was the other tower, and they all were still anxiously waiting, eyes glued to the set, holding their breath.

The chief started to read out the names. I didn't even listen. There was no point. It wasn't going to be Mr. Bennett. It couldn't be Mr. Bennett.

I wanted to walk away, but I couldn't. I was frozen in place, waiting for all of them to hear what I already knew, knowing that the hope they were all feeling was going to be washed away in just seconds. I closed my eyes and waited as each name was read out—each name I knew wouldn't be Mr. Bennett's.

I counted as each one was named. When the last one was read out there was a hushed silence in the room, as if people were still waiting for his name, or any name, to be said.

"And those are the names of the people who have been rescued," the chief concluded.

The kitchen erupted into tears, screams, sobs, and swear words as the truth sank in.

"Everybody, please!" Mrs. Bennett called out. "Please, everybody, could we all stop?"

The room quickly, instantly, became silent once again, except for the sound of the TV in the background.

"I'd like us all to gather in a circle."

A circle? What was she talking about?

"Gather in a circle and hold hands. I want to say a prayer."

Okay, that I understood. Besides, it would calm everybody down. We shuffled around until we formed a crude circle. I had my mother on one side, and she carefully took my sore left hand, while I offered my right to some guy on the other side of me. It seemed strange to hold his hand, but I did.

"Please, bow your heads," Mrs. Bennett said, and we all did. "Dear God, we pray for all those who have suffered through this great tragedy. We pray that You give them strength as thousands of people, like us, wait to hear about their loved ones. We know that from great tragedy can come great triumph. We have just witnessed the rescue of seven people, six of them men who were willing to sacrifice their lives to try to save the lives of others."

That's what firefighters and police officers did, I thought. They were the guys running up the stairs toward the danger while the rest of us were running away from it.

"And You have delivered them, spared their lives. We want to thank You for sparing the life of Josephine Harris, and for returning six husbands and fathers to their families. I can only imagine the joy in their homes right now."

I didn't need to imagine the sorrow in this one.

"I'd like to end with the prayer that the Lord taught us. *Our Father, who art in Heaven, hallowed be thy name . . .*"

CHAPTER
FIVE

Mrs. Bennett gave both of us a big hug and thanked us for coming, and then she handed my mother half a dozen muffins to take home. My mother tried to tell her it wasn't necessary, but she insisted. As we walked away, I turned back around. Mrs. Bennett was still standing at the door, a big smile on her face, waving. I waved back.

We climbed into the car.

"It's called 'denial,'" my mother said as she started the car.

"What?"

"Denial. She's pretending that nothing is wrong,

that everything will be all right. That's how she's dealing with it right now."

"It's just strange. Really strange. She seems so sure that her husband's going to be found. When Mr. Bennett wasn't one of the guys they rescued, she said that others being found only gave her *more* hope."

"Well, as long as they keep finding survivors, I guess there is *some* hope," my mother said.

"Some, yes . . . but for her it's not just a hope, it's a certainty. She's positive it's just a matter of time."

My mother pulled the car away from the curb. "Back when I was a social worker, I helped many people going through grief. We all deal with it in different ways."

"And pretending is one of them?"

"Not pretending. Denial. Until she knows for sure, James's mother has to believe in the best outcome. Maybe she feels she has to be strong for her children."

That did make some sense. Especially for Amanda's sake. She was pretty young, and it must have been even harder for her than it was for James.

"One theory says that there are five stages of grief and dying," my mother said.

"There are stages?" I asked, in disbelief.

"Death has been a part of life as long as there's been life, so we as a species have had to learn to deal with it."

"What's to deal with?" I asked. "You're alive until you're dead."

"That's about it for the person who dies, but not for the people who are left behind. According to the theory, denial is the first stage."

"What comes after that?"

"Anger, bargaining, depression, and then, hopefully, acceptance. How do you think James is doing?"

After the whole TV thing, he had gone back downstairs. I'd tried to talk to him, but he'd just said that he wanted to be alone.

"He's fine, I guess." Then I thought. "Maybe he's moved a little further on that stage thing," I said.

"Do you mean to anger?" she asked.

"Yeah." I wondered if she'd heard James smashing his guitar, but I didn't want to ask. I understood the smashed guitar, but I didn't necessarily think my mother would.

"Boys–men–often express their sorrow as anger."

"He is angry."

"That's okay, as long as he doesn't get stuck there."

"I don't think he will. He understands."

"And?"

"And he's doing what you'd expect. He's upset, crying, scared." I thought for a minute, then added, "James also said something about how he felt guilty."

My mother nodded her head. "He felt it was somehow his fault?"

"He thought that if he'd gone along with the crew instead of staying at the station he could have somehow changed how things happened for his father. Could that be part of that 'bargaining' stuff?"

"It almost sounds like a middle stage between anger and bargaining."

"What exactly does 'bargaining' mean?" I asked.

"It's sort of making a deal with God, or whoever. 'If my father lives, I'll try to be a better person,' or 'Take *my* life, not his,' or 'Let me have another five years and then I'll go peacefully.' Things like that."

"I don't think that's it. He just thought that he should have been with him, that he should have gone to the towers when his father went. And maybe now he feels like he should be down there."

"At Ground Zero?"

"Yeah. Maybe searching or helping, or maybe just being there."

"That makes perfect sense. It's part of making it more real. You remember Grandpa's funeral?"

"Of course." I was only nine then, but I certainly would never forget it.

"Do you know why we had an open casket?"

"I hadn't really thought about it." Back then, I'd thought it was just to spook me out. I'd never seen a dead person before. He was all pasty-white, and people kept saying stupid things like "He looks so natural." Unless they thought my grandpa wore makeup on a regular basis, there wasn't much that was natural about it at all.

"It's a common practice. Many people feel a need to see the deceased. They know in their heads that they're dead, but by seeing the body they can know in their hearts."

That did make sense, I guess.

"And it's still early for James's family, so I under-stand the difficulty accepting, but still . . ." She didn't need to finish the sentence because I knew what she was going to say.

"Do you know what I wish for James and his family?" she asked.

"That his father is okay?"

"Well, of course, but if he isn't, I just hope they find his body."

"You want him to be dead?" Now I really didn't understand.

"I pray that he's alive, but do you think he is?"

"How should I know?"

She turned slightly toward me just for a second and gave me that mother sort of look, like she knew I wasn't exactly saying what I knew.

"Okay, I know he's probably dead, but if they *don't* find the body there's still hope," I said.

"Hope is good. False hope isn't. Sometimes it's much better to know, to have closure and start the grieving process."

"But why wouldn't they find the body?" I asked.

"So far they're not finding a lot of bodies," she said. "The same force that twisted beams and pounded concrete floors into dust would cause a body to disintegrate." She shuddered. "I can't even think about that, though . . . not when it could have been you and your father."

I tapped her on the arm. "I'm here. Dad's in the house. We're fine."

"I know you're fine. It's just that there are other types of denial—"

"Whose car is that in the driveway?" I asked, cutting her off.

We pulled into the driveway. A car was parked right in the middle, partially blocking both lanes.

"I don't recognize it," my mother said. "Maybe it belongs to somebody from your father's office."

"Whoever owns it should learn how to drive . . . or at least park."

My mother carefully eased past to get up the drive and to the garage. She pulled the car up snug to the garage door and stopped.

I went to get out, but my mother placed a hand on my shoulder.

"Going to see James was a very caring thing to do," she said.

"He's my friend. My *best* friend."

"Sometimes people don't know what to say or how to act when there's a tragedy, so they just try to avoid the person, sometimes even good friends. James needs you to be there. So thanks for being able to do that."

"Sure, no problem."

I went to climb out again, and again she took my arm. "Just so you know, I'm here for you and for your father. Any time, twenty-four seven. If you need to talk you can call me or get me or wake me up in the middle of the night."

"Sure, twenty-four seven. I'll find you. I'm fine."

"You're going to be fine, but don't you get caught in denial either."

"I'm not in denial!" I protested. "I know that Mr. Bennett isn't going to be coming home."

"I mean about you and your father."

"What?" What was she talking about?

"About what happened to you and your father."

"It's just some stitches," I said, holding up my hand. "A few cuts. I got hurt worse than this when I broke my nose playing basketball."

"It was more than that. You two almost died."

"Yeah, and *almost* is the important word in that sentence. We *almost* died. But we *didn't*."

"But you *could* have."

This was starting to get really frustrating—why did she keep saying that? Was she *trying* to scare me? "Listen, Mom—we didn't die. I'm fine. Dad's fine. We're alive."

"That sounds like denial."

I tried to answer calmly—I figured if I sounded as irritated as I felt, she'd probably change her opinion and decide that I was all the way into the anger stage.

"I'm not denying anything," I argued. "I was there. I came down the stairs. I saw the buildings fall down. I know they could have killed us, but they didn't. I'm *fine*."

"Will, denial isn't necessarily about what actually happened. It's sometimes about what *could* happen in the future, or what might have happened but didn't. You almost died."

"Didn't I just say that?"

"You did, but it's as if you're downplaying the possibility, how close you came to dying."

"It doesn't matter if the bullet misses you by an inch or a mile, as long as it misses."

"No, I disagree. There's a big difference," she said. "And to not see that is to deny the reality."

"You're so wrong. If a bullet hits you, then the wound is there for everybody to see. If it misses you, no matter what the margin, you're just as *unwounded*. To think anything different is to deny the reality. Look, Ma, no bullet wound."

I held up my hands, keeping both palms turned toward me so she wouldn't be reminded of the stitches or cuts.

"Look, I was there," I said. "You were here watching it all on TV. Who do you think had a better view of what happened?"

"You did, of course."

"So, we're fine. Let's just leave it at that . . . We're *fine*."

"And I'm so grateful, so blessed. Just so you know, I'm here for you."

"I know, and if I find a bullet wound you'll be the first to know, I promise. Can we go inside now?"

"Of course."

Quickly I got out of the car and headed for the side door, my mother trailing behind me. I didn't want to give her any more chances to continue this conversation.

"Hello! We're back!" I yelled out as we walked in the door.

"I'm in the living room!" my father called back. "We're *all* in the living room!"

All? How many people were here? I figured he'd found some more people from his office. That was good.

"Will!" my father called out. "Come and say hello to our visitors!"

I wasn't really in the mood to talk to anyone.

My mother and I walked in. My father was sitting in the one of the wing chairs, facing us, and there was a little man–a Chinese man–in the matching chair beside him. I didn't recognize him, but then I didn't know very many of the people who worked with my father. As we walked into room the man stood up, a big smile on his face. And then I noticed a second person sitting on the couch. She was Chinese too, and she had two little girls sitting one on each side of her. On her leg was a large white cast. She smiled at me.

"Ting?" I gasped.

Her smile got even bigger. "I am happy again to meet."

"Ting insisted on coming over," my father said. "And this is her husband, Thomas."

The little man rushed over and took my hand and we shook. "I'm so pleased to meet you." His English was perfect.

"Um . . . I'm pleased to meet you."

"You're almost as big as your father," Thomas said. "Now I can see how you two were able to carry my wife down so many flights of stairs."

"It wasn't that hard," I said.

"I don't know how to thank you and your father for saving my wife's life."

"We didn't really do—"

"Please," he said. "We all know what you did."

"We were just lucky we heard her calling for help."

"*We're* lucky," Thomas said.

"It was unfortunate that nobody in her office realized she was there," my father said.

"I guess I sort of understand," Thomas said. "With all the confusion."

"It was more than confusion," I said. "The windows were blown out, furniture toppled, ceiling tiles and ducts down. It was like a war zone."

"We think it was one of those falling ceiling ducts that hit Ting on the head," my father added. "How are you feeling?" he asked Ting.

"Feeling?"

Thomas quickly spoke to her in Chinese, and she nodded. "Yes . . . better . . . head hurt and leg . . . hurt." She pointed at the bright, white cast.

"My wife's English is coming along," Thomas said. "We met when I was working in my company's Hong Kong office. Then I was offered a transfer back here— this is where my family is from—so we moved back a year ago. Ting started working at that office in the World Trade Center only two weeks ago."

"That might explain why people weren't looking for her when they left," my father said.

"Maybe," Thomas said. "The important thing is that you two did see her. Without you, I would have lost my . . . And my girls . . . they would have been without their . . . without their . . ."

"Your daughters are so beautiful!" My mother beamed.

Ting said something to the girls in Chinese and they stood up. "These are daughters," Ting said. "Mei-zhen and Ming-zhu."

Both girls curtsied. They were dressed in identical flowery dresses and wore matching black shoes and identical hairbands. With their shining dark hair and big eyes they looked like two little dolls. I felt so big compared to them.

"How old are your twins?" my mother asked.

Both girls held up four fingers. I would have thought they were younger because they were so small.

"Are they always this quiet?" my mother asked.

"Not always," Ting said. "Sometimes tell them to . . . sssshhhh!" she said, holding a finger in front of her mouth.

"Do you know what happened to the rest of the people in your office?" my father asked.

"We had a phone call from Ting's supervisor. They've located many people, but some are still unaccounted for," Thomas said.

"It could be days before you know for sure," my father said. "We're trying to locate people from my office."

Almost as if on cue, Suzie walked into the room.

"This is my right-hand woman," my father said. "Any more luck?"

"With tracking down people or locating an office?"

"Both."

"I just talked to Phil."

"That's great!" my father exclaimed. "I was worried about him the most." My father turned to my mother. "Phil had a big deal brewing, and I was terrified that he might have ducked into one of the floors, found a phone, and started working again."

"And Phil was speaking to Spencer," Suzie added.

"Fantastic. How many does that make?" my father asked.

"We know the whereabouts of sixty-seven people," Suzie said.

"That leaves us with thirty-two unaccounted for."

"I'll keep tracking. And I need you to make a final decision regarding a potential office. I have three sites, but we have to act fast. There are other businesses scrambling to find office space. New Jersey is going to become a very popular place."

"Never with me," my father added. "I've never forgiven them for taking away our New York teams. Bad enough that my beloved Jets have to share a stadium with those stupid Giants, but why does it have to be in New Jersey? That's like adding insult to injury."

"I don't think you can be mad at them for having the Meadowlands," Suzie pointed out.

"I don't have to be reasonable about this," my

father said. "This is sports, and reasonableness has nothing to do with . . ." He let the sentence trail off and a small, sad smile slowly formed on his face. "I guess what's happened really does make this sports stuff seem a little bit irrelevant, doesn't it?"

"It's always been irrelevant," Suzie said. "Glad you finally figured that out. So, I need you to make the final decision."

"We're obviously interfering with what needs to be done," Thomas said as he rose to his feet.

"No, no, that's quite all right," my mother said. "Please, sit down for at least a few minutes."

"Yes, we're so pleased that you came by. It was so nice of you," my father added.

"Regardless, I should be getting Ting home soon. She needs to rest," Thomas said. He went over and helped Ting to her feet. She almost toppled over, and he helped her to regain her balance.

"A broken leg and painkillers are a bad combination," Thomas explained as he passed Ting her crutches, still holding on to her with one hand. The two little girls clung to her on each side. I wasn't sure if that was helping to keep her on her feet or not.

"I was up all night checking on Ting because of her head injury," Thomas said.

"Every two hours," my mom said. "That's how I spent the night too."

"The night wasn't as bad as the day," Thomas said. "Waiting, not knowing my wife's fate, was far worse."

"I know how hard that was," my mother agreed. "We are both just so fortunate, so lucky."

"My luck was these two men of yours," Thomas said.

I felt myself blushing.

"It was such a pleasure to meet you," my mother said. "You have a lovely family."

"Thanks to your family," Thomas said. "Once all of this settles down, we'd like to take you all out to the best restaurant in the city."

"That would be wonderful," my father said. "But not necessary."

"It's just a small token, a nothing compared to what you've done for me, for us. Thank you."

He shook my father's hand and then mine. I offered Ting my hand. She took it and grabbed me, pulling me forward with such power that I almost toppled over. I couldn't believe that somebody that small could be so strong. She wrapped her arms around me and gave me a big hug.

"Thank you, Will," she whispered in my ear. "Thank you."

"You're welcome."

She released me, and then she hugged my father and my mother.

"I'll make sure we arrange to get together," my mother said. "Calling my husband would be a waste of time. He has no idea what we're doing or when we're doing it, but I'll arrange it."

"Thank you."

We walked them to the door, and once again they thanked us. It felt good but embarrassing. We stood at the doorway and watched as they got into their car, slowly backed out of the driveway, and started to drive away. Ting had her window rolled down and she waved, and we all waved back.

We closed the door and my father headed back into the den. My mother and I followed. Suzie was at my father's desk, on the phone. It sounded like a business call—something about getting computers delivered, but she didn't know the exact address right now. The man on the other end of the phone seemed to be giving her some trouble about that and she started talking about why they didn't have an address and why they needed the computers, and I could tell that his tone changed immediately.

"That was so sweet," my mother said. "Seeing Ting makes it all seem more real to me."

My father laughed. "Funny, it makes it seem more real to me to see it on TV," he said pointing at the set.

I looked at the scene on the screen. It was footage from yesterday. It showed both towers engulfed in fire, orange flames shooting out, thick black smoke rising up, staining the sky.

My father turned to me. "Does it seem possible that we were part of any of that?"

I shook my head. "I can believe we were there. I can't believe that any of it ever happened or that . . . Oh . . . my God."

Before my eyes the South Tower began to fall. It collapsed into itself and was swallowed up by the gray cloud that it produced. That cloud rose up as the tower disappeared completely from view.

"Wow," my father said, under his breath. "I've seen it a dozen times but it still seems unreal."

"This is the first time I've seen it," I said. I felt myself shaking. I hoped nobody noticed. I really hoped my mother didn't notice.

"That's the first time?" my father asked.

I nodded. And right then, even seeing it just once seemed like more than enough.

We watched as the cloud started to dissipate and the shadowy outline of the debris became visible. The smoky gray cloud obliterated the skyline . . . the whole sky.

"It collapsed straight down, but then fell to the front," my father said. "We went out the side. If it had gone the other way . . ."

He didn't need to finish the sentence. If it had gone the other way we would have been buried beneath it. We would have been dead.

I looked over at my mother. She was staring at the TV. She looked as though she was on the verge of tears.

The doorbell rang. "I'll get it," I said.

"I can," my mother said.

"No, you stay here," I said, as I went for the door. I was just grateful to get away from another bout of tears. My legs felt shaky as I walked.

CHAPTER
SIX

The doorbell rang again. Whoever it was, they weren't very patient. Probably somebody trying to sell us something. Or worse, somebody wanting to talk about what had happened to us. I'd have preferred a salesperson or a Jehovah's Witness, or pretty much anything else. I opened the door.

"James!" I exclaimed. "What are you doing here?"

He shrugged. "I just needed to get away from my place."

"I understand." After all, I'd just escaped my own living room. "Come on in."

"Are your parents home?"

"Yeah. Them and my father's assistant, Suzie."

He shook his head. "No, I don't want to come in. If I come in they'll want to talk to me. I don't want to talk to anybody." He paused. "Why don't you come out?"

"Sure, of course."

I went out and closed the door behind me. James sat down on the steps, and I sat down beside him. We sat there silently. James was a good enough friend that we could just sit together without talking. Well, usually. Right now, though, it felt kind of awkward. I had to say something, anything . . . preferably something ordinary, unimportant.

"Did your mother drive you over?"

"No. I'm not sure she even knows I left."

"You didn't tell her?"

"I went out through the back door. I just didn't want to be around all of those people."

"But what if she needs to get hold of you?" I asked. "You know, if they have to tell you something, or there's news . . ."

"I have my cellphone. I'll call her in a while. I needed to get away. I left just after you left and started walking, and then I realized I was right here."

"I'm glad you came over. Do you want something to drink, or are you hungry or . . . ?"

"I don't want anything. I just want to sit here for a while."

"Do you want me to shut up?"

"It's okay. I just don't want to bother you." He stood up. "Maybe I should go."

I got up too. "Are you going home?"

"That's the last place I want to go. I just want to walk."

"I could walk with you. That is, if you want me to."

"Yeah, that would be okay . . . that would be good," he said.

"Let me just grab my jacket."

"I'll wait out here."

I ran inside and grabbed my jacket from the hook. Then I thought maybe I should take along a couple of other things. I went to the kitchen to get my wallet and my phone. My mother was sitting at the table.

"I'm going out for a while," I said.

She looked worried.

"That was James at the door," I explained. "He's waiting out front."

"Why didn't you invite him in?"

"I did. He didn't want to come in. He just wants to walk, and I said I'd keep him company."

"That's nice of you. Where are you two going to go?"

"I don't know . . . No place, really . . . just walking."

"Can you do me a favor?" she asked.

"Yeah, I'll call and let you know that I'm okay," I said.

She smiled. "Am I that predictable?"

"Completely."

"I just need to know that you're fine."

"You always need to know that."

"Now more than usual. Just call, okay?"

"Do I ever not call?"

She gave me a hug. "You're a good guy."

"I try. I'll call."

I hurried out the front door and skidded to a stop. I didn't see James. I hadn't taken that long, had I? Where had he gone to, and how would I— I saw him standing a few houses down, leaning against a tree on the boulevard. I joined him.

"So, where to?" I asked.

"Nowhere special."

We started up the street. We were the only people out and walking. That wasn't unusual for my neighborhood. It seemed like sometimes the only people I saw out on the street were the ones who worked for the lawn-care companies. Everybody else was in houses or in their cars.

With school being canceled there probably should have been some kids around, but there weren't that many kids in my neighborhood to begin with. My mother called our area a more "mature" community. That just meant that the houses were so big and expensive that most of the owners had kids who were already grown up. There were a couple of kids that were my age or a little older, but hardly anybody younger.

James's neighborhood was only a dozen streets over, but it was completely different. The houses were smaller and there were always lots of kids. Funny how that worked: smaller houses equaled more kids; bigger houses equaled fewer kids. Not that we were going there. I didn't know where James was leading us, but it was pretty much in the opposite direction from his house.

"Cross over," James said suddenly.

"What?"

He bumped into me, and we abruptly crossed the street.

At first I wasn't sure why he'd done that, and then I saw the reason. There were some people coming down the street, and I figured he wanted to avoid them. That was probably the whole logic of going away from his house. The farther away we got, the less chance he'd run into somebody he knew.

"You hungry?" I asked.

"Nope."

"Thirsty?"

"No . . . well, maybe a little."

"How about a coffee?"

"I don't have any money."

"My treat. You can get the next one."

I wanted a coffee, and we both knew the best place to get one. But more important, I liked the idea of actually heading to a specific destination. I didn't like just wandering.

We cut through the park and headed down the main street. I was shocked by how quiet it was. There was barely any traffic, and a lot of the stores were closed. I knew that businesses in the city had shut down, but I hadn't really thought about the stores on our little main street not being open. I just hoped that didn't apply to the coffee shop . . . No, there were people at the tables and at the counter, waiting to be served. It was actually quite crowded. I guessed that even disaster didn't stop people from wanting caffeine.

James abruptly stopped in his tracks. "I don't want to go in."

"You can wait here and I'll bring it out."

He sat down on a bench.

As soon as I opened the door I knew he'd made the right decision. There was a TV on, tuned to coverage of what people were now calling "9/11." Since when had there been a television in here?

I joined the back of the line. Everybody in the whole coffee shop had their eyes on the screen. I didn't look. I just wished I couldn't hear, either.

The commentators were talking about the digging that was going on, looking for survivors . . . looking for people like James's father. I couldn't help glancing up at the TV. It was a live picture—that's what it said in a little box in the corner of the screen. It was beginning to look like a familiar scene. Smoke or steam was rising up from the twisted girders. Firefighters and men with yellow or white hard hats were moving through the debris, removing it, little by little. Flashing lights pulsed.

"And the search continues," the unseen announcer said. "The workers are now being aided by sonar devices, and rescue dogs, specially trained to smell people beneath avalanches, have been brought into service."

The scene changed to show one of those dogs. It was a Golden Retriever wearing a bright-yellow harness with a long leash attached . . . and what was on its feet?

"The dogs have been equipped with shoes so their paws are not burned," the announcer said, answering my question. "The metal remains hot as there are fires still burning below the surface."

"What can I get for you, son?" the man behind the counter asked.

I started back to the present. "Sorry, I was just watching."

"Hard not to watch. What will it be?" he asked.

"Two coffees, black, with two sugars each."

"No problem. It is hard to take your eyes off it, isn't it?"

"Yeah, hard."

"I'm just glad I was here and not there," he said.

"I was there."

"What?"

"Yesterday. Me and my father."

"Hey, Sam," he called out, and the other guy behind the counter turned to face us. "This guy was there yesterday."

"You were down in New York?" Sam asked. I didn't really know him, but I knew he was the owner of the place.

"Yeah, I was there."

"How close?" he asked.

"Right there."

"You mean . . . ?"

I nodded.

"Right in the World Trade Center?" he asked, incredulous. Some of the people at the counter turned to look at me, and I suddenly wished I hadn't said anything.

"Yeah."

"You mean *by* the towers?" he asked.

"In the South Tower, at my father's office."

"Hey," Sam called out, "you people hearing this? This kid was in the South Tower yesterday."

Now it wasn't just a feeling; everybody *was* looking at me. The first man came back with the two coffees and put them down in front of me. I offered him a five-dollar bill.

"Put your money away," Sam said.

"No, it's okay, I can—"

"Your money is no good here. What floor, kid . . . what floor is—was—your father's office?"

"Eighty-five."

"Isn't that above where the plane crashed?" he asked.

Before I could say anything, half a dozen people told him it was.

"Wow . . . you are one lucky kid."

"If I was lucky I wouldn't have been there to begin with."

"I mean you were lucky because you got out *before* the plane hit. That was really lucky."

"No," I said, shaking my head. "We didn't leave his floor until the plane crashed."

"What?"

I really didn't want to talk about any of this. Not here, not now, not to him, and not to this audience of strangers.

"Are you telling me that you got down through those floors where the plane crashed?" he asked.

"Yeah."

"*Nobody* got through those floors."

"Most of the people we saw did go up, but we didn't . . . We went down."

"Yeah, right," he said, and chuckled. "Look, kid, if you're going to make something up you should try–"

"I'm not making anything up!" I exclaimed. "I was there, in that building! And maybe it was luck or maybe it was something else, but I was there and now I'm here! And I don't want your free coffee!"

I threw the five-dollar bill at him, grabbed the coffees, and stomped out of the store, the coffees sloshing over the tops of the cups as I moved up the street.

James wasn't sitting on the bench. I skidded to a stop. Where had he gone now? I looked up and down the street. He was nowhere to be seen. I started to slowly walk and–

"Will!"

I turned. He was in an alley, leaning against a wall. I walked over and gave him his coffee.

"I saw somebody I knew coming," James said. "I just don't want to talk to anybody."

"I can understand that," I said. I was wishing I hadn't said anything to those jerks behind the counter.

"And I can't sit still," he said. "It feels like this isn't the right place to be. That I shouldn't be *here*."

"We don't have to be here. We can go any place you want," I offered.

"It doesn't matter. Wherever I am, I think I'll still feel the same way. It's . . . it's . . . I can't explain it."

I couldn't find the words to tell him that I thought I understood what he meant, but I did. It was sort of like being lost and not knowing the way out.

He started walking and I fell in beside him. We moved along the alley. It was probably a better place to be if we wanted to avoid meeting anybody. It was just us and the Dumpsters, garbage cans, and parked cars.

We walked past an open door, the back entrance to a store, probably leading into the storage room. Blaring out I could hear more reporting from a CNN announcer. James stopped walking and listened. I couldn't make out all the words, but I knew what he'd be talking about. There was no escaping it.

He turned to me. "How much money do you have on you?"

"I don't know. Thirty, maybe forty bucks."

"Can I have it?"

"Sure, of course you can . . . Why do you want the money?" I suddenly had thoughts of him taking off, running away.

"I know where I have to go."

"Where?"

"You won't understand."

"Where do you need to go?" I asked again.

He shook his head.

"I can go with you."

Again he shook his head.

"Look, I need you to tell me."

"Are you going to give me the money or not?" he asked.

I pulled out my wallet, and without even counting, took out what I had and handed it to him. It looked like about forty bucks.

"I'm going down to the city."

"To New York?" I exclaimed.

"Not just to New York. I'm going to Ground Zero."

"You can't do that!"

"I have to."

"Your mother won't let you," I said.

"I'm not going to tell her."

"But the city is practically closed down. Trains and subways are hardly running and—"

"I'll walk if I have to."

"James, even if you did get down to Manhattan, the whole area around Ground Zero is barricaded and restricted. They won't let you get near it." That was part of what I'd heard on the news.

"I'll worry about that when I get there. I have to try."

He suddenly started crying. I wrapped my arms around him, and he sobbed into my chest.

"I have to go . . . I have to go to where my father is . . . I have to."

"I know," I said. "I understand. But I can't let you go—"

He struggled free of my grip. "You can't stop me!" he said, a burst of anger driving away the tears.

"I'm not going to stop you," I said. "I was going to say I can't let you go *alone*. I'm going with you."

CHAPTER
SEVEN

"Yeah, I thought I should just check in," I said into my phone as I walked along the platform of the station.

"You know how much I appreciate that," my mother answered.

"No problem. We just got a coffee, and we're walking and talking."

"James probably has a lot of things he wants to talk about," she said.

"For sure. I think we're just going to walk around, maybe go to somebody's house. I'll check in when I can. But if it's a bad time—you know, if James is talking to me about something—then I might not

be able to call right then, or pick up if you call me."
I was giving myself a little wiggle room in case I
couldn't call because of where we were or what we
were doing.

"You know you can never call too often," she said.

"I know, I know, and you'll hear from me."

"Thanks. That's so important. Especially now."

"Sure. Of course. How's Dad doing?"

"He seems a little sad, but he's—"

"I meant about finding people. Has he found more
people from his office?"

"A few more. That helps a lot."

"And did they find an office?"

"Yes. Suzie's going out this afternoon to sign the
lease. Your father would have gone with her, but he's
waiting for the CNN reporters . . . Oh, you don't
know about that, do you?"

"No."

"Suzie thought that if your father went on CNN,
then he could ask the people they haven't been able
to find to contact him. So she called CNN, and they
wanted to talk to him anyway, so they're sending out
a team. They said that they'd really like you to be part
of that interview, too."

"I think I'll pass." Actually, I was more than fine
with not being a part of that. "I don't know when I'll
be home . . . you know . . . because of James. But even
if I was there I don't really want to be interviewed."

"Your father really doesn't want to either, but
Suzie's idea makes sense, and—"

"I have to go." I could now see the blazing white light of the train coming down the tracks.

"Just make sure you keep checking in . . . What is that sound?" She could obviously hear the train coming, and it was getting louder and louder.

For a split second I thought about trying to make something up, but then I decided I'd try to be honest for as long as I could.

"It's a train," I said. "We're by the train station. I've really got to go. Bye, I love you."

I hung up the phone before she could say anything else.

The train squealed into the station, and James suddenly appeared at my side. When the train doors huffed open we climbed in and took the first set of seats. It wasn't like we were going to have to fight for them. There were only a few other people on the whole car.

"Any problems with your mom?" I asked James. He'd been calling home at the same time I was.

"Nothing. She just wanted to make sure she could get hold of me. I told her my phone was on if she needed to call. What did you tell your parents?"

"It was my mom. I just told her that I was with you and we were walking around."

"That's not a complete lie. We will be walking, as soon as we get off the train."

The train started to move, and I felt a shiver go up my spine. I knew that going to the city was wrong, but I knew it would be even more wrong to let James go by himself. There was no sense in even thinking about it now, though—we were on the train and heading downtown. Well, I could always get off at the next station if I really wanted . . . No, I couldn't do that. We'd go downtown, find out that we couldn't get anywhere close to Ground Zero, and then we'd head back. And really, what was the difference between us walking around there and walking around here? Not that my mother was likely to see it that way.

I looked at my watch. It was just a few minutes past one. If everything went the way it should we'd be back by four, five at the latest. We'd be back before anybody could discover where we'd been. There was no way I wanted my parents to find out. Especially not my mother. I knew that she'd be worried about my going into the city even under normal circumstances. But really, what could happen? It wasn't like the towers were going to fall down again.

"Thanks for coming with me," James said.

I changed seats so that I was sitting opposite, facing him. "You'd do the same for me."

"I would. But you must be trying to figure out why I want to do this," he said. "You must think I'm crazy."

"I don't think you're crazy."

"That's good, because I don't think I could explain it to you, you know, put it into words."

"I think maybe I know why you need to go."

"You do?"

I nodded my head. "I think so."

"So?"

I took a deep breath before starting. I wanted to make sure I said it right. "I was down there yesterday," I began. "I was *in* the building. I almost died, and now, today, I'm watching it on the TV and it doesn't seem real. It's like some bad made-for-TV movie." I paused again and thought carefully about what to say next. "You need to go down there because for you *none* of it seems real."

"None of it," he agreed. His voice was barely audible above the noise of the train.

"You need to go down there to see."

For a split second I almost mentioned what my mother had said about open caskets to see the dead person, but I caught myself in time. There was no point in talking about dead people or caskets or funerals.

The train started to slow down as we came into the first station. There were only a few people waiting on the platform. It came to a stop, the doors opened, and we waited as nobody got onto our car.

"I've never seen it like this," James said. "You know, almost nobody on the train."

"Yeah, it is pretty empty."

The doors closed and the train once again started moving. I stared out the window. It was then I noticed that it wasn't just the train that was empty. Like our neighborhood, here, too, the streets were almost empty, stores and schools and businesses closed and dark. It was like there was some sort of holiday . . . although it was nothing like a holiday. I was going to say something about it to James, but he was staring intently out the window and I didn't want to bother him.

The door at the far end of the car opened and the conductor came in. He stopped at the first man, took his ticket, punched it, and then returned it to him. There were so few people that he wouldn't have much work to do today. He quickly worked his way along the car until we were next.

The conductor looked as if he hadn't slept. His eyes were red and he had a stubbly beard—he obviously hadn't shaved.

"Tickets, please," he asked.

James continued to stare out the window. He hadn't heard or noticed the conductor.

"James," I said, tapping him on the leg.

He turned to face me. He looked unsure, confused. He glanced up at the conductor but it was like he didn't understand who he was or what he wanted.

"He wants our tickets."

"Tickets? Didn't you get the tickets?"

"Me? I gave you all my money, remember?"

"Oh, yeah, right."

"So you boys don't have tickets," the conductor said.

"No, I'm sorry. We each thought that the other one had bought them," I tried to explain, but it sounded pretty lame even to me.

"I've heard that story more than a few times," the conductor said.

"It's not a story, honest!" I suddenly had visions of us being arrested or given a big fine—they were allowed to fine us about five hundred dollars each. "We could pay you now," I pleaded. "James, give him the money."

The conductor shook his head. "Keep your money. Today, it's okay. Hard not to be distracted. Don't worry about it."

"Thank you so much. It won't happen again."

"It's not worth worrying about. Not with everything that's going on. What stop are you boys going to?"

"Grand Central," I said.

"And from there?" he asked.

"We're going south."

"That could be a problem. The subways are running off schedule, and some of the lines have been closed down completely. Better to go on a surface route, take a bus. Besides, I'd be nervous getting on a subway right now. You know, they could be targeted."

"Targeted for what?" I asked.

"Lots of rumors. Who knows what the terrorists are going to try to hit next?"

I felt a rush of fear surge through my body. I hadn't thought about any of that. Yesterday we'd heard rumors of other attacks but nothing had happened. Of course, that didn't mean something couldn't happen today. People were talking about America being at war against the terrorists who'd done this, and it seemed like we were living in a world now where anything, absolutely *anything*, could happen.

"How far south are you going?" he asked.

"Down close to the bottom," I said, without saying exactly where.

"Can't get too far down. The whole southern tip has been barricaded off. It's restricted to emergency personnel."

"Thanks. That's all good to know."

That's what I'd figured. And maybe now that James had heard it himself we could just turn around and go home.

"Take care, boys," the conductor said. He started to walk away and then spun around. "I was just wondering, *why* are you boys going into the city today?"

I clearly knew the answer but I didn't know what to say, or what I *should* say to him.

"The authorities have requested that anybody who doesn't need to be in the city stay away," he told us.

"We have to go," I said.

"Yeah?" he questioned.

"Yeah," James said. "My father is down there. He's a firefighter."

"Your father is one of New York's bravest?" the conductor said.

James nodded.

"In that case, I have something for you two." He took his pad and scribbled something on it. He ripped off the sheet and handed it to James. "You boys don't need to buy a ticket on the way back, either. If you get stopped by a conductor you just give him this."

"Thanks," James said.

"No. Thank you, and thank your father. Good luck, boys."

CHAPTER
EIGHT

The train went underground as we got close to Grand Central, and the car got dim. I suddenly started to feel anxious all over. My chest began to tighten up, and I could feel my stomach starting to churn. That was stupid. I'd been on this train a hundred times, and a hundred times I'd entered the tunnel leading into the station, but now, today, I just felt unnerved . . . I couldn't help thinking about those people who had been underneath the towers when they collapsed, the people in the concourse or in the subway below. Most of them would have been killed, but some of them might have been trapped. Right now, they'd be waiting for rescuers. I couldn't even imagine the terror of lying there in the dark. Praying . . . waiting either to be found or to die.

When the train glided into the platform and light spilled in through the windows again, the darkness and that anxious feeling went away as quickly as they had come. The doors opened and we went out to the platform along with the other passengers. There couldn't have been more than twenty of us on the whole train. There was a strange quietness. It wasn't just that there were so few of us, but also that nobody was talking. There was no noise. I could hear my feet against the platform as I walked.

Up ahead I could see two policemen waiting at the platform exit, stopping each person who tried to pass. They were looking through briefcases and purses. What were they doing that for? We joined the back of the line and shuffled forward. As we got closer I started to overhear what was going on. They were searching people, looking for weapons, looking for explosives.

It was hard to argue with that. To a terrorist, Grand Central Station, the transportation hub that connected New York City with every other town and city on the map, would have looked like a promising target. On ordinary days, there had to be hundreds of thousands of people passing through. But did I look like a terrorist? Did that woman they'd just searched, or the elderly man in line next? On CNN they'd said that the terrorists were sixteen men—four each from the two planes that hit the World Trade Center, the one that attacked the Pentagon, and the one that went down in Pennsylvania—all from the Middle East. None of the people here on the train looked like they were . . . Well, that man three up from us did have a darker complexion. He could have been Muslim.

I watched as he was searched. I was close enough to hear some of the questions and answers. He didn't seem to speak much English, and I was sure that they were taking longer to search his bag than they did the purse of the lady ahead of him. Finally they let him go. The next two searches took almost no time and we were up next.

"Hey, boys," one of the officers said.

"No parcels or packages, right?" the second officer asked.

"No, nothing," I said. I opened my jacket so they could see underneath.

"Go through," the first officer said.

"Thanks."

We moved along the corridor toward the big hall.

"Can you believe that?" James asked.

"I guess they just want to make sure. I've heard that a lot of people are worried about another attack."

"Yeah, I know," James said. "That's why they grounded all aircraft. They were afraid another plane was going to be hijacked."

"Like the four others."

"Those people in Pennsylvania, they fought back," James said.

"It didn't help them."

"But it did help the people on the ground. I just wish the passengers or crew on the first two planes had fought. Maybe the towers wouldn't have been hit."

"The people in those two planes, especially the first, they didn't know what was going to happen. Who could have imagined that?" I said. I kind of felt as though I had to defend them.

"I guess nobody," James admitted.

"And even if they had known, they hardly had any time to react," I added. "In the fourth plane they had more warning."

"They knew they were probably going to die," James said, "but they were heroes. They made sure nobody else would die."

"They *were* heroes." I paused. "Like all the firefighters and all the police officers."

We walked into the Great Hall of Grand Central. Both of us stopped walking and gawked at the sight. I'd been in Grand Central a hundred times and I'd never seen it like this. It was silent and practically empty. And of the few people who were there, most weren't commuters passing through. Police and soldiers were all over the place. They were at every exit in pairs and groups. The soldiers were in fatigues with helmets and packs, and they were carrying rifles or machine guns.

"This is so unreal—it's like an army movie or something," James said quietly.

"I guess it should make me feel safe . . . but somehow . . ." I shrugged.

"Yeah, it's sort of unnerving."

"I guess this would be a natural target."

"I don't want to think about it. I don't want to even try to think like a terrorist. Let's just get to the bus."

We moved across the hall. I looked away from the soldiers and up to the painting of the constellations on the ceiling. I always thought that was so cool. We passed under the watchful eye of four soldiers standing at the door. They didn't seem that interested in people leaving the building, but they were searching everybody who came in. They let us go without a word or a second glance.

We went through the door and onto the street. There were more soldiers holding rifles at some of the intersections. Except for the soldiers, the sidewalks were almost deserted, as were the roads, which held nothing more than a few taxis.

"Where do we catch the bus?" I asked.

"I'm not sure. When I come in it's usually with one of my parents. How about if we just start walking south?"

"It's got to be seventy blocks."

"We won't have to walk the whole way. We'll just go down Park Avenue. We'll look for a bus while we're walking," James said. "Besides, I can't just stand and wait. I have to keep moving."

"I guess that's better."

We started south and crossed 42nd Street—we hardly had to look; there was virtually no traffic at all. It was so *un*-New York.

"Can you smell it?" James asked.

"Yeah, it's like somebody is burning garbage. The air is even a bit hazy."

"This is New York," James pointed out. "The air is always a little bit hazy."

"I guess you're . . ." My phone rang and I started, stifling a little yelp. I fumbled for the phone and pulled it out of my jacket. "Hello?"

"Hello, Will."

"Hi, Mom."

"You were going to check in," she said.

"It's been less than an hour," I said.

"Oh, yeah, you're right." She sounded genuinely surprised. This had better not be a new phase, I thought, where she needed me to check in every hour like I did when I was twelve. That wasn't going to be happening.

"I was just about to call," I lied.

"I just wanted to make sure you're all right."

"I'm good."

"And James?" she asked.

"My mom says hello," I said to James.

He nodded and waved.

"Oh," my mother said. "He's right there, so you can't really talk about him . . . right?"

"Right. And James says hi to you, too."

"Are you still just walking?" my mother asked.

"Still walking." It was nice not to have to lie.

"Do you know when you'll be home?"

"Can't really predict that right now." Again, that

was the truth. "I gotta go. Talk to you later." I flipped my phone down and hung up.

"Maybe you should call your mother," I said to James.

"Probably should."

He pulled out his phone and took a seat on a bench. I moved off to the side. I wanted to give him some privacy. There was no telling what news he might get.

I looked to the south. I knew we'd traveled only a few blocks and were a long way away, but still, I thought maybe I'd be able to see something. Maybe if I moved into the center of the street or went to the boulevard in the middle, I could see farther. I stepped out onto the road but jumped back when a loud horn jarred me. A gigantic truck with a crane on its back was coming down the road. I'd been so distracted that I hadn't even thought to look. I watched as it rumbled by. I expected the driver to make some sort of obscene gesture, but instead he waved and gave me a little smile. That was really strange—a polite driver in New York. He had to be a visitor to the city.

Behind the truck there were two smaller vans—workmen's vans—and a large truck with glass sheets on the side. I started to pay more attention to the vehicles that were on the road. Aside from the taxis, most of them were like those that had just passed, service vehicles. That all made sense. Most businesses were closed down, but tradespeople would have more work than they could possibly handle. Lots of buildings had been damaged, and there had to be shattered windows in almost every building for blocks around Ground Zero.

James was still on the phone. Was his mother giving him a hard time for taking off? Or maybe he was being told something bad about his father . . . and there was nobody here but me. What would I say to him?

Then I heard a loud, rumbling sound. I looked up and down the street. I didn't see anything along the road that could be making that sound . . . It wasn't on the road . . . it was coming from the air . . . It was an airplane! My gut instantly tightened. How could there be an airplane? They'd all been grounded! If there was a plane in the air it could mean only one thing . . . another attack!

"James!" I yelled out. Before I could say another word the plane—no, planes—came into view. Three fighter jets, F16s, streaked overhead. Not terrorists. U.S. Air Force planes. They were flying overhead to protect us. I felt instant relief. But like the sight of the soldiers on duty it was also disturbing. Who would have thought that we would need the military overhead to protect us?

"They are pretty impressive," James said. He'd hung up the phone.

"Can you imagine flying one of those?" I asked.

"I can. I could see myself as an air force pilot."

"I thought you were going to be a firefighter," I said, the words coming out before I could stop myself.

"Things change. Firefighters protect people. Our military protects people too. It's the same job with different equipment. Maybe one is more needed than the other right now."

I didn't know how to respond to that, so I decided not to. "Things go okay on the phone?"

"Yeah. She wants me to come home soon."

I knew what I wanted to know next, but I didn't know if I should ask. I took a deep breath. "Any news?"

"Nothing *but* news," he said, "but nothing about my father, if that's what you mean."

"Yeah, that's what I mean. I guess no news is good news. That's what my nana used to say."

"I guess that makes sense . . . for a while, anyway. Then no news is just no news."

Another conversation I didn't want to have.

"Here comes a bus!" James said.

I looked up the street. A transit bus was coming toward us. James waved his hands, and the bus slowed down to pick us up.

CHAPTER
NINE

"This is the end of the line, boys," the driver said as he pulled the bus over to the curb.

I looked over at the signs at the intersection: Broadway and Canal. The end of the line wasn't that close.

"Sorry I can't get you farther," he said. "This is as close as the authorities are letting us go."

"How far is it from here to the towers?" James asked.

"Twelve, maybe thirteen blocks, but you probably can't get there."

"We can't?"

"The whole area, for at least four blocks in each direction, is barricaded. It's restricted to authorized personnel only."

I'd figured that was going to be the case from the beginning, so I wasn't surprised. This would be the end of the line for us, as far as we could go, as close to Ground Zero as we could get. I wasn't troubled by that. I was encouraged. I knew James needed to see it. I also knew that I didn't. Seeing it on TV was almost too much for me. Instead, we could stand by the barricades for a while, look in, leave, and get back home. We *needed* to get back home. How much longer could I keep my mother guessing about where I was?

We climbed off the bus. The air was thick and hazy. The smell that had been building throughout the ride was now so strong that I could almost taste it in my mouth. The closest I could come to describing it was that it was like somebody having a big barbecue and throwing last week's garbage and a full set of snow tires on the grill.

Wordlessly we walked down Broadway. There were more people on the sidewalk here—moving both toward and away from Ground Zero—and lots more vehicles on the street. Along with the police and fire vehicles and ambulances were a lot of vans with writing on the side and more tradespeople. There were carpenters, plumbers, electricians, and welders. Among the vans was another truck with one of those big cranes. They must have been using those to remove the girders.

I looked at my watch again. It was almost two-thirty, well past lunch.

"You want to get something to eat?" I asked James.

"I'm not hungry."

I was, but I wasn't going to say anything about it right now. Besides, there really wasn't any place to eat. All the little restaurants that littered the area were closed. The stores along Broadway and down the side streets were, without exception, barred and shuttered.

Up ahead I could see that the road was blocked off. There were big yellow barricades, manned by police and soldiers. Crowded around them were dozens and dozens of people. I assumed that they had wanted to get closer, like us, and, like we were about to be, they'd been blocked.

We wandered into the back of the crowd. Despite the large number of people there was complete silence. Everybody stood stock-still, almost as if they were in some sort of trance, staring toward where the towers would have been if they'd still been standing. From here we would have been able to see them . . . at least, I was pretty sure. Now all there was to see was smoke rising up into the air, adding to the haze that was already hanging over everything.

It was then that I noticed the photos. A woman was holding a picture of a man. Underneath was his name and some information and in big letters "HAVE YOU SEEN HIM?" She was here looking for somebody who was missing. Beside her was a man holding a picture of a woman above his head, turning it slowly from side to side so everybody could see her. She looked to be the age of somebody who could be his wife. Again there was more writing, asking about her whereabouts.

I understood then that these weren't people who were here to gawk or try to catch a glimpse of what was happening. These were people like James— people who had lost somebody, or at least couldn't find somebody, somebody who was important. They were down here with photos and pleas, hoping against hope that someone could help them. I felt a bit like an intruder, like I'd wandered in to some stranger's birthday party or . . . no . . . I'd wandered into somebody's funeral, and I didn't know the person and I wasn't invited. Then I looked at James. Okay, maybe I *was* invited.

Slowly we shifted through the crowd, moving closer to the barricade and— I stopped in my tracks. The whole side of a wall was covered with those pictures and pleas. There were dozens and dozens and dozens of them. But why wouldn't there be that many and a whole lot more? That was how many people were missing.

Beneath the pictures were flowers, hundreds and hundreds of flowers, in bunches and singles. There were lit candles and stuffed animals and signs with big letters naming the person in the picture and offering information about them and who to contact if they were located.

There was a knot of people standing off to the side in the plaza and we walked toward that group. As we moved closer I could see the reason for the crowd. There was a camera crew interviewing people. We kept moving closer until we were near enough to see and hear what was going on.

A man stood in front of the camera, holding up a big picture. It showed a woman in her twenties with dark hair, dark eyes, and a big smile.

"This is my daughter, Marcia," he said. He had an accent and darker skin, and he looked like he was Mexican or Cuban or something like that.

"She's very beautiful," the female interviewer said.

"She looks like her mother. She has her mother's eyes," he said.

"And your daughter, your Marcia, she worked in the World Trade Center?"

"In the North Tower. She worked in the restaurant at the top of the building. She called home after the plane crash," he said. "She left a message on the answering machine. She said that she was fine, that she was safe. I wish I'd been there to talk to her instead of just hearing her voice on the . . ." His voice cracked and then trailed off, and it was obvious he was fighting back tears.

"You haven't heard from her since then?"

"Nothing. Nothing," he said, shaking his head. "Marcia, we know you're okay," he sobbed. "We haven't given up. Anybody who has heard . . . please call us . . . please." He started to cry even harder but kept holding the picture up for the camera.

One by one people came forward to the camera and held up pictures of the person they loved—the person who was missing. All these different people, but pretty much the same story. All were desperately hoping to hear something, anything.

The announcer—she was young and pretty and seemed vaguely familiar—looked directly into the camera. "These ordinary citizens, these ordinary people, are here hoping, praying for word on their loved ones."

I thought she was going to start crying. Not fake, movie-star, made-for-TV crying but genuine tears. She sniffed and wiped her eyes.

"They have gathered here, as near as possible to the spot they last heard from, or of, their loved ones, but this is as close as they can get. Their way is blocked by police barricades—"

"I can't watch this any more," James said. He practically ran away, pushing past people.

"James!" I called out, but he didn't turn around or slow down.

I rushed after him, but he was moving fast. I bumped past the people in my way and grabbed him from behind by the arms.

"James, I . . ." Then I started to cough, and instead of stopping it got worse and worse, and it felt like it was caught in my throat and I couldn't breathe.

James slapped me on the back. "Are you okay?" He sounded worried.

I nodded my head, but I couldn't answer or stop coughing.

He slapped me harder on the back. "Just sit down," he said, and he eased me to the curb.

"Does anybody have any water?" he called out.

Almost instantly half a dozen water bottles were thrust toward us. He grabbed one—a full one—twisted off the cap, and handed it to me. I took a big swig and swallowed, and it washed the cough back down my throat.

"You okay now?" he asked.

"Yeah . . . I'm . . . okay."

I noticed that we were in the middle of a little throng of people. I coughed again and took another swig of water.

"I couldn't stop and I couldn't catch my breath," I tried to explain, although I hardly had enough air in my lungs to answer.

A woman kneeled down in front of me. "I'm a nurse. Do you have asthma or bronchitis?"

I shook my head.

"It's all the stuff in the air," she said. "God knows what we're breathing in."

"I guess."

"Are you feeling better?"

"I'm not coughing," I said. I was suppressing the urge to cough.

"Good."

She took my hand, turned it over, and placed two fingers against my wrist—she was taking my pulse. Thank goodness she'd taken my right hand, the one that had only a few cuts. I didn't have the energy or the oxygen to start to explain to her what had happened to my other hand.

"A little fast, but you'll be fine. Sit there for a while. If you start coughing again you'll need to talk to a paramedic."

"I'm good, honestly!" I protested.

She turned to James. "You're his friend?"

"Yeah."

"If it gets that bad again you'll have to get him to see a paramedic, understand?"

"I don't need a—"

"I'll make sure he does it," James said, cutting me off. "I'll make sure he's okay, whether he likes it or not."

"Thanks. It's good to have a friend."

She walked away, and James sat down beside me. We sat there as the crowd slowly dissipated and we were no longer the center of attention. I continued to sip from the bottle. I took a big drink and spat it out on the pavement . . . That's when I noticed that there was something, some kind of dust or powder, that had accumulated on the ground. It was so fine that it looked almost like snow . . . I knew it was from the collapse of the building. Concrete or pulverized paper or . . . I didn't even want to think about what else it might be. That was the same stuff that had gotten into my lungs and was now making me cough so badly.

"I shouldn't have brought you down here," James said.

"You didn't bring me. I came because I wanted to come."

"No, you didn't. The last place in the world you want to be is here. You came because you were being a friend."

There was no point in arguing. We both knew it was true.

"It's time for you to get home."

"Sure," I said. I felt a sense of relief. I looked at my watch. "With any luck we should be home by–"

"Not *we*. *You*."

"What are you talking about? We should both go home."

"I'm not going home. I came here to get to the towers, and I'm still going down to the towers."

"But the barricades . . . what that woman said . . . They aren't letting anybody get any closer."

"I have to get through," he said.

"James, they're not letting anybody through."

"You go home. I'm going to find a way." He got to his feet.

I jumped up and took him by the arm. "I'm not going home without you."

"Well, I'm not going home," he said.

"Then I'm not going either."

"No, really, you should go. I'll be fine," he said.

"*We'll* be fine. Maybe I can't make *you* come with me, but you can't stop *me* from going with you. Come on, let's find a way in."

CHAPTER
TEN

We figured that the most congested places would be around the barricades on the major streets coming down on the north side of the restricted area, so we started to circle around to the bottom. With the ferries not running there would be almost no one coming up from the tip of the island. Almost instantly we knew we were right. The crowd at Beekman Street was smaller than at Broadway. We passed by Ann Street, and then John and Maitland. As we continued to circle, each street had fewer people than the last. That was encouraging. Of course each street also still had a barricade manned by police officers.

We were also noticing more evidence of what had happened. The streets were filled with scrap paper, blowing and swirling and accumulating in little pockets where the wind could deposit it but not blow it away. Some of the buildings had smashed and broken windows, and down one street there was a bunch of cars with their roofs caved in and windshields smashed. It was too far away for it have happened right there, so I figured that they'd been towed. They were probably starting to move the cars that had been crushed away from the site.

The smell was also becoming worse and the air seemed thicker. We were moving downwind, and the fumes were being carried toward us. The burning garbage smell was becoming something worse than that . . . stronger, more putrid and heavy, like burning sewage.

We crossed over Courtlandt. It was, of course, barricaded too, but I looked beyond the barricade. There, in the distance, I caught my first glimpse of the outline of the remains of the towers. Twisted, blackened metal poked out of a pile of debris, while smoke rose up into the already hazy air. I stopped and my heart seemed to skip a beat, sending a chill down my entire body. That was all that remained.

"That's . . . that's it," James said.

"That's it." It was hard to believe. We weren't seeing it through the lens of a TV camera. Here it was, big and ugly and smelly, and the smoke wasn't just in my face or my eyes, it was in my nose and in the pores of my skin.

We walked forward, eyes fixed on the wreckage, toward the barricade and the two policemen who were manning it. Both of them were wearing surgical masks. I wondered if that would block out the smell somehow. We stepped aside as a city van came up from behind us. The two officers pulled the barricade aside to let it enter. James quickly walked toward the opening.

"Hang on a second!" James called out. "We need to get through!"

He caught me off guard, but I quickly fell in beside him as he walked toward the barrier. He'd impressed me.

Unfortunately, the two police officers didn't feel the same way. One of them swung the barrier back into place and the second stood there, arms folded across his chest, blocking our way.

"We need to get through," James said again.

"This gate is for authorized personnel only," the officer said.

"We are authorized. This is the gate we were *told* to come to. This is Courtlandt, isn't it?"

I had to hand it to James. He sounded not just confident but a little bit cocky—like, the *nerve* of them to interfere with us!

"And just who told you to come to this gate?" the second officer asked. Again, he didn't seem as impressed as I was.

"A police officer. I didn't get his name, but I do know he had three stripes on his sleeve . . . which is three more than either of you two."

One of the officers pulled down his mask. "Look, kid, we can't just let people wander into the site."

"Nobody here is doing any wandering. We're here to help."

"Just how old are you two boys?"

"We're both eighteen," James said.

Okay, that was a bit of a stretch. Maybe we could have got away with seventeen, but eighteen . . . ?

"Vehicle," the second officer said again.

We all turned around as a big black car came toward the barrier. One officer brushed us off to the sidewalk and the second went up to the driver's window, which glided down. I couldn't hear what they were talking about.

The back door of the car opened up and a man climbed out. He was wearing a white hard hat with a suit and tie, the tie hanging loosely around his neck. He looked exhausted. He also looked kind of familiar. He shook hands with the officer and they exchanged a few words, and then the man pointed at us and they said a few things more. What were they talking about, and what would any of it have to do with us?

As the man walked toward us, the second officer actually saluted him! Whoever he was, he was important. He shook the officer's hand.

"How's it going, son?" he asked the officer.

"As good as can be expected, sir."

Sir—he had to be somebody high up in the police force. That was why he wasn't wearing a uniform.

"Hello, boys," he said then, and we both mumbled back a greeting.

This was not good. We'd got somebody important involved with us. This couldn't possibly end well.

"The officer says you want to get into the site," he said.

"Yeah," James said.

"Yes, sir." I thought being formal wouldn't hurt. Besides, if the two guys with the guns were calling him that, who was I to disagree?

"You must understand our need to keep the area restricted. For safety and organizational reasons, we can't let just anybody—"

"We're not just anybody," James said, abruptly. "We *need* to get in."

The man looked at James and then at me. His look was long, and instead of the anger I'd expected him to show James for cutting him off he looked thoughtful and sad. Everybody looked sad today. He also did look *incredibly* familiar. I must have seen his picture in the papers before or something.

"It sounds like it is important. Tell me, why do you need to get there?"

"It's my father," James blurted out.

"Your father was in one of the towers?" he asked.

"He was there," James said. "He's with Ladder Company Fourteen."

"Your father's a firefighter." He sounded concerned, and there was something about his voice—he even sounded familiar.

James just nodded. I could tell he was on the verge of bursting into tears again. I think the man could tell, too. He put an arm around James's shoulders.

"And you haven't heard from him?" the man asked. James shook his head.

"You know we're doing everything we can."

"I know," James said, his voice wavering. "I just want to go down and help . . . I need to be able to help."

The man turned to the officers. "These boys are eighteen?"

The two officers exchanged a skeptical glance. "That's what they're telling us, sir."

Were they buying it? Because if they asked for ID it would be game over.

"Then they're allowed in on my authority, okay?" the man in the suit said.

"Of course, sir!"

"No problem, sir."

"Good. Send them over to St. Paul's. Radio over and tell them to make sure they have masks and gloves."

"Will do . . . Right away."

"What's your name, son?"

"James Bennett."

He shook James's hand. "And your father?"

"Samuel . . . Sam."

"And you, son, what's your name?" he asked me.

"Will Fuller."

He reached out and shook my hand, and I winced slightly. He looked confused and then took my hand

and looked at it. That's when he noticed the stitched-up gash on my other hand.

"How did you get those cuts, son?"

"I got them yesterday."

"Not *when*, son. *How*."

"Here," I said softly. "I was here."

"Here?"

"In the South Tower."

He looked surprised, shocked, and concerned.

"I was here with my father."

"And your father . . . ?" He let the sentence trail off, but I knew what he was asking.

"He's at home now. We got out before the collapse. Just before. I got all cut up when it fell."

"That's . . . that's a miracle. It's stories like that that help me get through the day." Then he turned back to James. "My thoughts and prayers will be with you and your family."

He spun around and headed back for the car before we could say anything in response. He jumped in, and one of the officers quickly pulled the barricade out of the way. The car glided by. We waved, but because of the tinted windows we couldn't see if he waved back.

"St. Paul's is one block in and two blocks north," the officer told us.

"Thanks."

"Oh, and by the way, if you're not really eighteen, I don't want to know about it. Eighteen will get you into the site, so stick with that story."

"Yeah," the second officer agreed. "If you'd told us in the beginning why you needed to be here we might have let you in. Firefighters and police, we might fight among ourselves, but we're still all family . . . especially now."

"Thanks."

We walked past the barrier, but then I thought of something, so I stopped and spun around.

"That man, the one in the car, who is he?" I asked.

The two officers looked at each other and burst into laughter. That was about the last thing I'd expected. I didn't know what was so funny about that question but now I certainly felt stupid for asking it.

"You don't know who that is?" one of them asked in amazement.

I shook my head.

"Me neither," James said. I appreciated his sharing my stupidity and admitting it out loud, even if it wasn't true.

"That was the mayor."

"Mayor Giuliani?" I gasped. Of course it was—that was why he looked so familiar.

"We've only got one mayor," the officer said.

"And thank God we've got the one we've got," the second offered. "He's been everywhere since this happened. The man has been a tower of strength."

The second nodded his head in agreement. "So, if anybody bothers you, you just tell them that the mayor—that *Rudy*—said you should be here, that you

have to be here."

"We'll tell them," I said.

"And boys, our thoughts are with you as well."

Both officers took off their hats and saluted us. That was as unexpected as the laughter. For a moment I froze, not sure how to feel about it, until James grabbed me by the arm and pulled me through the gate—there was no way he was letting this chance slip by.

CHAPTER
ELEVEN

With each step forward we were moving closer to
Ground Zero. We were walking straight toward it– the
wreckage, the few parts that remained standing,
looming larger and larger overtop of us. I should have
been glad for James: he was getting to where he
needed to go. Instead, I felt that same sense of dread
that I'd felt in the train tunnel coming into Grand
Central Station. My whole body was tingling and my
legs felt a little wobbly, and I was finding it harder and
harder to take a deep breath. Was the air that much
smokier here?

Worse, I couldn't seem to stop my mind from

rushing back to yesterday. It just felt wrong to be moving in this direction. My instincts told me that I shouldn't be walking *toward* the towers, I should be running away, and doing it as quickly as I could.

"This is all unbelievable," James said. "But I guess it must look familiar to you."

"No, none of it," I admitted. "You know, except for what I saw on TV."

"But you were here."

"When the tower collapsed we were caught in a cloud of white dust. I couldn't see three inches in front of my face. And even when it cleared I wasn't looking back. I was focusing on moving forward and getting the hell away from here."

"You know, you don't look so good," James said.

"What?"

"You don't look so good . . . You're all white."

I really wasn't feeling all that great. My whole body felt hot and I was shaking and struggling to draw in a breath. It was like my chest was tight and my lungs couldn't open up.

"You should sit down," James said.

I didn't argue or fight as he helped me slump down onto the doorstep of a small store.

"Drink some more water." He took the bottle from my hand, unscrewed the top, and gave it back to me. My hand was shaking as I took a sip. I deliberately slowed down my breathing.

James sat down beside me. I liked that better than having him hovering over me.

"You didn't sleep much last night, did you?" he asked.

"Probably about as much as you. It's the air here . . . I can't breathe too well."

"We need to get masks like the cops had," James said. "You were saying about all the stuff, that cloud that you were in yesterday. That must be why you're coughing so much, why you're having trouble breathing."

"Yeah, that's it, that's got to be it."

"Do you want to stay here while I get us both masks?"

"No!" I practically yelled. I grabbed him by the arm as he tried to get to his feet. The last thing in the world I wanted was to be alone. "I'm better. I'm fine."

Slowly, unsure, I got to my feet. I wasn't nearly as shaky. I was probably a little bit better.

James got up as well. "You really don't want to be here, do you?"

I didn't want to lie to James, even if I could have got away with it. We'd been friends so long we knew each other inside and out.

"If it were me, having gone through it, what happened to you, I sure as hell wouldn't want to be here."

"But you would have come with me anyway, right?" I asked.

"I'd have tried. I just don't know if I'd have the guts. I think I'd be scared."

"No, I'm not scared," I said, defending myself. "I just feel . . . I don't know . . . sort of uneasy."

"I can't imagine what it was like," he said.

"No kidding–I was *there*, and *I'm* having trouble imagining it," I said. "I've been trying to figure out how to explain it to people . . . how to put it into words, and I think maybe now that I'm here, standing in its shadow, I know."

"Well?"

"This is going to sound stupid."

"Like this will be the first time you sound stupid?"

My mouth dropped open, and then James smiled and laughed, and for a split second none of this seemed real and we were somewhere else–somewhere normal.

"Go on," he said.

"This whole thing is like a movie . . . like one of those cheap, screamer/slasher/monster movies," I said.

"Okay, you're right . . . that does sound stupid. So, explain."

"I'll try. You know those movies where there's this awful monster or killer or something like that, and until it kills the first time nobody sees it coming? There's a bunch of kids and they're at a party, or at the beach or camping. Just having fun."

"And the killer strikes out of the blue," James said.

"Exactly. And then, once people see it, they somehow manage to escape."

"But not really," James said. "They just *think* they've escaped."

"Right. And it keeps coming after them, and finally, somehow, they manage to kill it, and everybody takes a deep breath."

"Which is always a mistake," James added.

"Yeah, because it's not dead and they're not safe."

"And somebody else is killed," James said. "Usually one of the secondary characters. Either the not-nice guy or the girl who isn't quite as hot as the others."

"Exactly."

"Standard horror/slasher movie. But how does this relate to you?"

"I was in my father's office yesterday. What could be safer or more boring than that?"

"And then the plane hit the tower."

"The *other* tower. We saw the monster, but we were fine. We weren't in any danger. They even told us that over the P.A. Then the second plane hit our building. But it didn't kill us. And after that we had to go through the fire. But we survived that, too. We got all the way down and out of the building."

"You escaped the monster. You were safe," James said. He *did* understand where I was going with this.

"Then it came after us," I said. "The building collapsed and almost got us."

"But again you escaped."

"Next, the second building collapsed, and we had to run again to escape the cloud of debris that was hissing out and chasing us again." I paused. "And finally, everybody kept talking about another plane, or car bombs, or maybe something else. We just kept looking over our shoulders for the monster to reappear."

"And now you're back, and you see the dead body of the monster, but you're still wondering if the monster is really dead?"

"Stupid, huh?"

"Not really. I think it all makes sense. I remember seeing this homemade video on one of those TV shows and there were these four guys who caught this gigantic shark. They hauled it out of the water and it was lying there on the dock. It had probably been out of the water for over an hour, and it sure looked dead to me. And that's when it bit one of the guys. Right on the butt."

I laughed. I was surprised, but I did.

"You know," James said, "if this *is* like a monster movie, you must be the one guy who never gets killed."

"Me?"

"Sure. You're the guy who lives to tell the story. You're Bruce Willis, Sylvester Stallone, Wesley Snipes, and Mr. Mission Impossible all rolled into one. You're bulletproof."

"Do you think?"

"Why not? They have to keep you alive for the sequel."

"That's what I'm afraid of."

"What do you mean?"

"I'm afraid that today is the sequel."

"We won't let that happen. Besides, I should be more worried than you."

"Oh yeah? Why's that?"

"Because in those slasher movies it's always the slightly more handsome, funny best friend who gets it in the end. And, of course, that's me."

"I don't think you have to worry about that."

"Oh, and here's something else. In those movies the bad things happen only when people leave the group and go off somewhere all by themselves," James said.

"That's so true! Don't you feel like yelling at them, 'Don't go into the basement by yourself, you idiot! You're going to die!'? But they won't listen."

"So, here's the deal. You keep an eye on me, and I'll keep an eye on you," James said. "Let's make sure that neither of us is alone. Now, you ready to get going?"

I nodded. I was ready. We started walking again. I was keeping an eye on James, but I was also keeping an eye on the carcass of the monster. I looked at the collapsed buildings, getting bigger and bigger as we moved toward them. Actually, there was no way I could have looked away even if I'd wanted to.

"There's a lot of damage to all the buildings on this street," James said.

He was right. In the buildings we passed, more windows were broken than intact. Some were blown completely out, and curtains billowed in the breeze. Many of the lower windows had already been boarded up, but the ones higher up that still held shards of glass looked as if they had jagged teeth glistening in the light. What would happen if those fell when we were below? We'd be cut to ribbons, sliced open, maybe even decapitated. I moved off the sidewalk and onto the street, pushing James with me. It wasn't like we had to worry about traffic.

On the road was a thicker layer of the same dust we had passed through earlier. It was like walking through snow—gray, dirty snow that fluttered up as we passed, swirling into the air. This was the same stuff that had spilled out of the buildings and into my lungs when that cloud overwhelmed and engulfed us after the collapse. Again, I didn't want to think about it.

Ground Zero was covered in a haze of smoke that both clung to the ground and rose up into the sky. The rubble was still piled high. In some places, the skeletal remains of the towers—twisted metal girders and the latticework of the facing—stood seven or eight or ten stories high. What had been distinct buildings were now just jumbled, tangled, and twisted pieces all stacked on top of each other. It looked so much larger than on TV—but that's how I had to think about all of this, like I was just watching it on TV, not standing here in person. I had to try to put a filter between me and this place. But could I do that?

We moved off to the side of the street when we heard a vehicle, another one of those big crane trucks, come up behind us. As it passed I noticed the license plate—it was from Pennsylvania. I'd heard that they were getting extra police and firefighters and paramedics from all over, so it wasn't surprising that construction people were coming from all over as well.

All around the site there were dozens of vehicles. Some were on the move—with flashing lights and beeping back-up signals. Others were just hulks that had been smashed and burned and were still covered in debris. We passed a gigantic fire truck covered with ash and dust; the front windshield was cracked, the roof caved in, and it looked as though it had burned. How ironic was that? I noticed that James deliberately kept his eyes averted so he couldn't see it.

Police cars, ambulances, and fire trucks were outnumbered and outsized here by dozens and dozens of dump trucks and gigantic cranes. There were still a lot of police and firefighters, but many, many more people were wearing yellow or white construction helmets. It was those hard hats that stood out. They looked like little white and yellow dots moving through the wreckage.

"This way," James said, taking me by the arm. We turned to the right and our view was obstructed now by smaller buildings that were close to the site but seemed to have escaped the damage. I just wished I'd been sheltered by their walls when the South Tower fell. Between the buildings I could still catch glimpses of Ground Zero, just for a second or two, and then it would disappear again. I liked it when it was gone.

In front of the church, St. Paul's, there were dozens and dozens of vehicles. These were mainly the usual assortment of emergency vehicles, but among them, tucked in beside the church, were three big motor homes. One of them had "COMMAND CENTER NYC PD" written on the side. There were also at least ten or eleven transport trucks neatly parked at the curb.

The church was old and worn and tucked in among the tall buildings. A large tree on one side had been shattered, almost split in two, and it was leaning now against the wall of the church. Strangely, remarkably, the big stained-glass windows of the church were intact. How could that be? Buildings all around the church, and some a lot farther away from Ground Zero, had *all* their windows smashed. Were stained-glass windows stronger? Or was it some sort of religious thing, like God protecting the church? If it was, why hadn't He chosen to protect those people in the towers instead?

We circled around the church, and I caught sight of the graveyard that sat at the rear. I'd known it was there, but I'd forgotten. Old, worn tombstones were surrounded by a wrought-iron fence. I'd always thought it was strange to have a cemetery in the middle of the city, dead people trying to sleep in the hustle and bustle of the Financial District. Now it seemed like the most natural thing in the world.

We walked up the path toward the church door. This was clearly a place where the volunteers helping at Ground Zero were gathering. Some were sitting on the steps, some were slouched down against the wall. Many of them were wearing overalls or uniforms, with hard hats or police caps or firefighters' headgear on their heads or resting beside them. They all either wore masks or had them loosely lowered onto their necks. Some were eating, others were drinking. Their faces were uniformly dirty. Strangest of all, without exception, not one person was talking. They were all just there, silent, staring, or eyes closed. It was so eerie to walk down the path among them.

We went through the open door of the church and were instantly greeted by a different scene. The pews had all been pushed to the sides and the church had become a command center. People in suits and uniforms were standing in groups talking. There were boards and maps and a bank of telephones, all in use or ringing, needing to be answered. In the back corner was a lineup of people, bowls and plates in hand, waiting to be served a meal. The odor wafted across the room—it drove away all the other smells and I suddenly felt hungry. Other than breakfast, I hadn't eaten anything today. But I knew I couldn't just line up for food. Those guys had done something to deserve it.

Up against the wall there were two gigantic television sets, both turned to CNN. On the screen were images of the scene right outside the door, and people were sitting or standing and staring at those images. How bizarre. They could have looked out the door and seen the real thing, but they were transfixed by those electronic images that anybody could see, anywhere in the world. Maybe that was the attraction. They were protected, the reality safely behind the glass screen. They could pretend that it was happening somewhere else, or that *they* were somewhere else. I could certainly understand those feelings.

The scene on the screen changed to a completely different image. It was a replay of a speech given by the British prime minister, Tony Blair. I'd already seen it. I was too far away and the volume was too low for me to hear, but I remembered what he had said—that this wasn't just something that had happened to us, wasn't just an attack against Americans. This was an attack against all people who believed in freedom, and his country was standing with us. That meant something. We weren't alone. We had friends. We had allies. His speech ended, and the scene shifted again to an interview with a firefighter.

That was the other thing about watching the news. It was like when my dad and I had been in the stairwell, yesterday. We hadn't really known what was going on, and here, now, we still knew only a little slice of the reality. The news was showing us more than we could see with our eyes.

"You two here volunteering to help?" a man asked.

"Yes, sir," James said.

Volunteer? I'd thought we were just coming here to watch, to see what was going on, and—

"You two look pretty young."

"We're eighteen," James said, very definitely, looking him straight in the eyes.

The guy furrowed his brow like he didn't really believe us, but I guess they weren't looking to turn away fresh, rested volunteers. "Okay, sure. Go through that door and get gloves and masks and goggles. And you'll both need safety boots before they'll let you on the site."

"We don't have boots!" I pointed out. Finally, a reason why we couldn't go any—

"No problem, they'll fit you with boots as well."

"Great. Thanks," James said.

"Those shoes of yours—they look like they'd be good for basketball, but they'd just melt out there."

"Melt?" I asked.

"There are a lot of hotspots in the debris. Rubber-soled shoes like you're both wearing would turn into hot rubber goo. Get your equipment and come on back, and you'll be assigned to a work gang."

CHAPTER
TWELVE

"I want to thank all of you for coming down here to offer your help," the man said. He was wearing a suit, with a tie hanging loosely around his neck, and he had a yellow hard hat perched on his head. He was an older guy, and he looked dead tired.

James and I were standing in a group of about twenty people. We now all wore masks, gloves, boots, and overalls that they'd given us. My new, expensive Adidas were in the trailer where we'd changed. Those trailers were filled with donated supplies for the people working at the site. I looked around at the group we were standing in—we were clearly the youngest people there, but considering that volunteers were supposed to be at least eighteen that wasn't a big surprise.

"Let me start with the basics. Once you leave this building you all *must* stay together as a group. You *must* go only to the assigned areas. You *must* listen for instructions at all times." He paused and took a sip from a water bottle he was holding. "You'll be working in two-hour shifts. At the end of that shift you'll come back in here, eat and hydrate, and rest."

"What if we want to stay out longer?" one of the men in our group asked.

"That's not an option. You'll have a chance to go back out, but only if we feel you can handle it. We can't have people out there who are tired.

"Now, to the best of our knowledge, it is presently safe on the site, but that does not mean there aren't some possible dangers."

"What sort of dangers?" one of the men asked.

"The debris pile is not completely stable. As we are removing materials it could become increasingly destabilized. That's why it's important for you to stay on the line, exactly where you are placed. If you think you see something important off the line, then you call for assistance, and a rescue crew will be dispatched to investigate."

I was convinced—I'd make sure to stay exactly where they put me.

"There is also a danger that one or more of the surrounding buildings could, potentially, collapse."

James looked over at me. I knew what he was thinking. *The monster might not be dead.*

"They have been surveyed, and our engineers assure us that while some of them will eventually need to be torn down, they do not present any imminent risk of collapse. Regardless, if you hear a call to evacuate you drop whatever you're doing and leave, quickly, and go to the safety areas you'll be directed to."

If they wanted me to leave they wouldn't have to say it twice. But according to James I didn't have to worry–I was bulletproof. Even if there was a sequel to the movie, I was going to survive it to star in the next.

"At all times when you're outside you need to keep your goggles and your mask on," he said. "This is important, especially the mask. We don't know exactly what's in the air, but we do know that there will be contaminants of all kinds, including asbestos, lead, and other heavy metals, and concrete dust. We're all here because we want to help, but you help nobody if we have to rescue you, or if your health is adversely affected. Now, before we go out I want everybody to drink a lot of water–we need to stay hydrated–and, this is important, everybody, either leave your cellphones here or turn them off."

Problem: if I turned off my phone and my mother tried to get in touch with me she'd panic. There was only one thing I could do. I'd phone her now, and then hopefully she wouldn't try to get in touch with me until I was back in and could turn on the phone again. Right after that, after we'd done our shift, we'd be heading home. We *had* to head home.

"We'll meet at the far doors in two minutes," he yelled out, pointing. "Get lots of water now—get hydrated!"

The group scattered. Lots of people were pulling out their cellphones and either making last-minute calls or turning them off.

"We have to call home," I said.

"I was thinking that," James said.

"I don't know how much longer we can keep them from knowing that we're here."

"I was thinking that as well," he agreed.

"We're good for a couple more hours. After this shift is over, though, we'll have to think about it, about going home. Okay?"

"Okay."

I was relieved. I'd expected a fight.

We headed for a quieter corner of the church. I just hoped I could block out the noise or it would be hard to explain. I dialed, and my mother picked up on the first ring.

"Will?"

"Yeah, it's—"

"I was trying to call you, and I couldn't get through!" She sounded a bit freaked out.

"I guess we were in a dead zone." I remembered how hard it had been to get calls out of this area yesterday, and I wondered if some of the cellphone towers had been damaged or destroyed, or if there were still too many people here trying to use them.

"Where are you?" she demanded.

"We're walking."

"By this time you could have walked to New York."

I almost gasped. "Probably there and back," I said. "But that's what James needs, so that's what I'm doing."

"Can you be home by four?"

"Um . . . maybe . . . but probably not."

"It's just that the CNN crew is coming over and—"

"Mom, I'm not doing any interview."

"But they really want both your father and you."

"I already said, I'm not talking to anybody. I get why Dad wants to do it, though, to help contact people from the office. Has he made any progress?"

"He and Suzie have tracked down almost eighty people."

"So they have to find only about twenty more."

"I'm afraid it isn't that simple. They've already been in touch with family members of most of those twenty. They . . . they're . . . missing."

"Like James's father."

"Like him and almost two thousand other people," she said.

"Hopefully they'll find them."

"It's good to be hopeful, but it's best to be realistic," she said.

"What do you mean?"

"So far today they've rescued only twelve people from the rubble."

"Yeah, but if there are two thousand people missing they have to be finding somebody . . . even if they're just finding . . . finding the . . ."

"Will, we talked about this. They think that most of the bodies will never be found. The announcers are saying that the few remains they're recovering are . . . The bodies they do find are broken, or burned up, consumed by the flames. The rest are nothing but dust."

Dust, the dust I'd been breathing in, choking on.

"I don't want to hear any of this!" I practically yelled. People turned around to look at me. I turned away and lowered my voice. "Sorry."

"It's okay. I understand."

She could say that, but she didn't, not really. Not just because she didn't know where I was right now, but because she couldn't possibly understand what I'd gone through.

"Okay, everybody, let's go!" the crew foreman yelled out.

Had she heard? "I've got to go," I said, before she could question me. "I'll call you when I can."

I pushed the End button and then the Power button, and the phone chimed out a message that it was closing down.

We all assembled around the crew foreman.

"I'd like you all to put your masks on now," he said. I took one more big breath before slipping it over my face. I adjusted it so that it fit snuggly over my mouth and my nose and took in another breath. It was harder to get the air into my lungs. I guess that meant that it was doing its job. Coming down from the tower, my father had taken a necktie, torn it in two, and given it to me to put over my mouth and nose. This was similar, but at the same time very different.

It was so hard to believe that that was only yesterday. It was so hard to believe that it had been real to begin with. I just wished that my father were here today. No, that was wrong. I really wished that I *wasn't* here, that I was with my father at home.

James and I settled into the middle of the pack as we headed out. I had to fight the urge to step out of the line. I didn't want to go out there. It was strange, but today, for the first time in my life, I understood how a church could be a sanctuary, one I didn't want to leave.

Even through the mask the foul, burning smell outside became much stronger. We circled around the side of the church, and Ground Zero stretched out before us. Any thought that this wasn't real, any glimmer of disbelief, was finally washed away. I stopped, and James immediately bumped into me from behind.

"You okay?" he asked.

"I'm good. I'm good." I started moving again.

We marched right up the center of the road. Whatever had been in the way had already been hauled off to clear a path for us.

We entered the plaza. This was familiar to me. This was almost exactly where I'd been when the tower collapsed. This was where I'd crawled away. I was shocked by how much it was littered with chunks of concrete—some the size of small cars, and others just the size of baseballs. Any of those pieces could have crushed my skull. But none of them had. I was bulletproof.

We passed a large dump truck that had backed in as close as it could to the edge of the rubble. Stretching away from it was a long line of volunteers. Small pieces of debris and buckets were being passed hand over hand, and the two men at the end of the line joined together to throw the debris into the back of the truck. This scene was being played out in half a dozen places, lines of volunteers working doggedly to clear endless piles of small pieces.

We shuffled along beside the line. I decided it was best not to look up or around. I needed to watch where I was walking. I kept my eyes on my feet, moving carefully over the uneven, shifting ground. As we continued to move forward the foreman started to remove people from the line and replace them with us, the fresh hands. He'd skip over a dozen people before deciding who to remove. This wasn't what I'd expected. I'd thought James and I would at least be working side by side.

Finally I was next.

"You take a break," he said to a man in the line. Wordlessly he stepped out.

I didn't need to be told what to do. I just took his place. James tapped me on the shoulder as he passed by, following the foreman. Before I could even say goodbye to James the man in front of me turned around–he was holding a piece of concrete. For a split second I just looked at him, wondering what I was supposed to do. Then I nodded a greeting, took the concrete, and turned to pass it to the man behind me. He gave me a nod. I was part of what needed to be done.

It didn't take long to settle into the rhythm of the job. Piece after piece–concrete; drywall; wood; small pieces of metal; some melted, molded, nearly unrecognizable bits of plastic–came through my hands and was passed toward the truck. If the pieces were small enough they came in buckets . . . Full buckets were dumped and the empty ones were passed back up to be refilled. There wasn't much conversation except for an occasional warning: "It's hot," or "Heavy," or "Sharp edges." I focused on the work, thinking about not thinking, but it was impossible to ignore what was going on around us.

While we were moving the smaller pieces there was bigger work going on. Girders were being cut up. The flare of the blowtorches sparkled blue and orange in my eyes, and then the giant pieces were lifted out by cranes and loaded onto flatbed trucks to be hauled away. Sometimes the girders would swing almost overtop of us, and I'd feel myself involuntarily leaning away.

Sometimes my mind would start to think about what *might* have been. A few seconds later, a longer stop on a floor, a slightly slower pace and we wouldn't have made it out in time. Or maybe I would have made it out and my father would have died. Or we both would have died. Or I would have been trapped underneath the wreckage. It might have been me they were digging for right now . . .

I felt those anxious feelings start to creep in, and my chest became tighter, my breath came harder and faster. I couldn't let that happen. I forced myself to think about the task instead. I tried to forget about what was all around me and what might have been, and instead thought only about the single piece of steel I was passing, or the concrete, or the bucket. The next piece was handed to me—a sharp hunk of metal. I took it from the man in front of me. That was the only part of this that had to concern me, the only part I needed to worry about. I turned around and handed it to the man behind me. Maybe I couldn't handle the whole thing, but I could handle this one little piece . . . and then the next . . . and then the next . . . and then the next. I felt myself start to relax.

Moving throughout the site were the rescue workers. These included soldiers—I was told they were rescue specialists. Some of them wore headphones and were holding listening devices, trying to pick up faint sounds from underneath the wreckage. I didn't know how they could hear anything faint with so much commotion around them.

Strangest, though, were the dogs, like the ones I'd seen on TV, the avalanche dogs that had been trained to pick up the smell of humans buried under snow. Here they were trying to pick up the presence of people trapped beneath concrete and steel. The dogs wore little white boots on their feet to protect them from the sharp edges and the heat. The ground where I stood was cool, but two men had come down the line having to replace their boots, the soles re-formed into a bizarre waffle of melted rubber.

There were also firefighters all over the site, working with large poles, probing the wreckage. Others had hoses and were watering down the spots that were still alive with smoke from flames beneath the debris. The smell was tremendous, and depending on the way the wind was swirling we would, from time to time, become engulfed in smoke. The mask helped, and it seemed to stop me from breaking into another coughing fit. The goggles protected my eyes from the wind that whipped up ash and dust against exposed skin. It felt like hail pelting against my face.

I watched those firefighters working. So many of them looked like James's dad. They were about the same height, same mustache, same build—I kept thinking that I was seeing him. Was James thinking the same thing?

He was five places ahead of me in the line. Occasionally I would catch a glimpse of his face or the back of his head. Even though our eyes didn't meet and we didn't exchange a glance or a word, it was reassuring to have him close by. I wondered what thoughts were going through his mind. It was probably better I didn't know.

A signal went out for silence. This meant that the searchers thought they might have found somebody—

something. Slowly, a ripple of silence spread out until the entire site was hushed. People stood perfectly still. Trucks were turned off, cranes stopped, torches extinguished, and no one spoke. We all collectively held our breath.

The first time that happened I'd waited expectantly for what was going to come next, figuring that it surely meant somebody was about to be pulled from the wreckage—either dead or alive. But nothing happened that time, and we were given the signal to start working again. All over the site silence slowly gave way once more to the banging and crashing of work. It happened again, another four or five times, and eventually it started to seem more like an excuse to stop working and rest. I really needed to rest.

My arms were sore and I was dying for something to drink. I felt exhausted, physically and emotionally. I just wanted to sit down, or lie down, maybe close my eyes for a few minutes, go to sleep. Sleep would be nice . . . but not here, at home. Soon we could go home, and I could go to sleep. I looked down at my watch. It was only five in the afternoon and I really wanted to go to sleep.

This time at least I could see where they were digging. The ironworkers and the rescue workers were side by side, carefully removing chunks of metal, shifting the debris, trying to dig down. A call came down the line. They wanted a stretcher to be brought up! That could mean only one thing—they'd found somebody! A ripple of excitement radiated throughout the site. This was why we were here–this was why we were all here. I tried to think, Could it be Mr. Bennett? Were we on a part of the site where the South Tower had collapsed? There was no way for me to know that.

Two paramedics brought a stretcher up and set it down beside the rescuers. I was there, watching, hardly breathing, waiting, hoping, and praying. Was it possible that I'd been a little part of moving some of the pieces that had allowed somebody to be saved?

The rescuers and paramedics reached down–they were taking somebody out of the hole and placing him or her on the stretcher and . . . No . . . it was too small to be a firefighter . . . Was it a child, or . . . ? It wasn't a person . . . it was part of a body. I looked away.

CHAPTER
THIRTEEN

The stretcher holding the body bag was carried right past us. There was an American flag draped over the body. Each person took off his hat, or helmet, holding it at his side or over his heart as the stretcher passed by. I did the same. Police officers saluted. There wasn't a sound. Just the silence of respect.

I looked up at James. His eyes were on the ground. I wanted to go up and talk to him, offer some words of comfort, but I didn't have any to give. The stretcher was loaded into a waiting ambulance. The doors were closed, and it started to pull away. There was no siren, no flashing lights. No need for either.

Coming up the line was a foreman, and trailing behind him were fifteen or twenty people who were going to replace those of us on the line who were ready to step out.

"Anybody need a break?" he called out.

I needed a break, but I knew I couldn't leave James there alone. I looked over at him and . . . His hand was up! There were five or six other people with their hands up too. I thrust mine up.

"Okay, son, go and get some rest and some water," he said as he gave me a pat on the back.

"Thanks, sir."

"You've worked hard."

I stepped out and a replacement took my spot.

"Thank you," I said.

He nodded.

I walked back down the line. The bucket brigade hadn't stopped, and pieces were already coming back down to the truck. I reached over and took a large piece of concrete from one of the men as it was being passed down the line.

"I'm going down anyway," I said, and he mumbled something through his mask that I couldn't understand.

It was harder to walk with the weight, but I didn't want to abandon the job and the people doing it without taking one more piece. I came up to the dump truck. It was almost full. I'd need to really heave it to get it to the top of the pile. I didn't know if I had the strength left in my arms to do it.

"Let me help."

It was James. His face was covered in sweat and dirt and soot.

"I'll take one end," he said. "On three."

We swung it. "One . . . two . . . three!"

We both strained as we flung it up and onto the top of the truck, where it landed with a loud thud.

"Let's go inside," I said.

"How you feeling?" James asked.

"Tired. Really tired."

My whole body was exhausted, but I wasn't shaking. It was almost as if I'd had the shakes worn out of me. My legs were dragging as we walked. All I wanted was to get inside, take off the mask and goggles, and get something to drink, something to eat.

As soon as we entered the church I pushed down my mask and took a deep breath. "That feels good," I said.

James had removed his mask completely and put it and his goggles into his helmet. I pulled mine off as well.

Then I started to pull off my gloves. The right glove came off easily, but the left was stuck and hurt as it came off—as I peeled it off. Then I saw the reason why. One of my stitches had broken open and my hand had been bleeding. The blood had congealed into the glove, but now that I had pulled it free, my hand was bleeding again. I held it up in the air and examined it. It was funny, but I had the sensation that it wasn't *my* hand I was looking at.

"You'd better have somebody look at that," James said.

"I'll go to the clinic near my house as soon as I get home."

"You'd better have somebody look at it before that."

I turned to James. "But . . . but we'll be home in a couple of hours."

"I want to go out for another shift . . . or two."

"That's not what we agreed to," I said. "We have to go. I can't keep stalling my mother."

"You don't have to stall her any more. You can just go home."

"We already talked about that. I can't leave you here by yourself."

"I'm not by myself," he said. "Look around."

"You know what I mean."

"I know," he said. "Look, let's just get something to drink and sit down and talk about it, okay?"

I nodded my head. I did need water, but I wasn't sure what there was to talk about. We needed to go home. *I* needed to go home. It wasn't just because of my mother. Those anxious feelings had been getting harder to fight, and I wasn't sure if I could force myself to go back out there again.

We joined a line of people waiting to get food and water. I had to try to think of what I could say to James to convince him that he had to come with me. I couldn't leave him here by himself, but I really couldn't stay any longer. I was caught. If I thought about it, though, I did have a way out, guaranteed. We really were too young to be here. If I wanted to,

I could just pull out that ace in the hole and tell somebody we were only fifteen. They'd have us out of here in a second. But I couldn't do that. It wouldn't be fair to James. On the other hand, was James's breaking our deal and refusing to come home fair?

We each grabbed a tray and shuffled forward. There were women behind a counter, and they put bottles of water—two each—and sandwiches onto our trays.

"What happened to your hand?" one of the women asked.

I looked down at my hand; it was bleeding onto the tray. "It's nothing," I said. "A stitch broke open."

"You have to have that taken care of," she said.

"I told him that," James said.

"It's just a little blood."

"It's more than a little blood. I'm a nurse. Let me see it."

Reluctantly I put down my tray and held out my hand.

"These stitches are fresh," she said.

"They were put in yesterday."

"What happened?"

"I'm not sure, exactly."

"It happened here," James said. "He was here yesterday."

"And you're back for a second day to help? Good for you."

"I wasn't here to help yesterday. I was here when it happened. I got that when the tower collapsed. That and these cuts," I said, showing her my other hand.

"You were here?" She sounded amazed—no, awed. "What was it like?"

"It's hard to describe . . . hard to even understand."

"You probably don't want to talk about it," she said.

She was right. I didn't. Talking about it meant thinking about it. In my head, I wanted to pretend that I hadn't even been here . . . *Denial* . . . I wanted to deny that I'd been here. Maybe there was more to what my mother had said than I was willing to admit.

"You have to be really careful with that hand," she said. "You need to worry about it getting infected. Go and see one of the doctors. He'll clean it out and stitch it back up."

"I'll do that as soon as—"

"As soon as you finish eating," she said, cutting me off.

"You should," James agreed. "Even if you're leaving, it would be easier than going home, explaining it to your parents, and then going out to the clinic."

I shrugged. I guess that did make sense. "I'll have them look at it," I agreed.

"How old are you boys?" she asked.

"We're eighteen," James said.

She eyed us suspiciously. There was that ace in the hole, staring me in the face. All I had to do was "accidentally" blurt out that we were really fifteen, and she'd gasp and then tell somebody and they'd escort us off the site. James wouldn't have a choice. Then the decision would be made for us. And it really would be in James's best interests and . . .

No, I couldn't do that to him. I wasn't going to say a word.

"Well, boys, you two go and enjoy your food, and you get that taken care of right away. I've got my eye on you," she said, looking squarely at me. "If you don't see a doctor I'm going to be angry, and you don't want to see me angry, do you?"

"No, ma'am."

"Good. Now go and enjoy your food."

"Thanks."

I looked down at the cellophane-wrapped sandwich. I didn't even know what type it was. Actually, I didn't care. I was so hungry I wasn't sure if I was going to unwrap it or eat it cellophane and all.

We wandered off and found a spot in a corner that was empty. It was one of the few places in the church that wasn't taken. We slouched down against the wall and took a seat on the floor. James took the wrapping off his sandwich. I was hungry, but I wanted water more than food. I took a big slug from the bottle. It was warm but wonderful, tracing a path down my parched throat. I tipped it back and chugged it down, emptying the entire bottle.

"Funny," James said, "this sandwich has no taste whatsoever."

"What type is it?"

ERIC
WALTERS

He pushed back the bread. "Ham and cheese. I just can't taste anything. It's more like a texture than a taste."

I unwrapped mine and had a look at it. It was egg

salad. I hated egg salad. I took a bite. I couldn't taste it either. "It's like my taste buds are all burned out."

I didn't have time to worry about that. We needed to sort this out. We needed to leave. "James, I'll have my hand taken care of and then—"

"Look!" James said, "On TV. It's the president."

On the screens along the church wall the president was standing behind a podium, giving a speech.

"I want to hear him," James said.

I didn't. All I wanted was to convince James to come home with me.

James got to his feet, and reluctantly, I followed behind. There was a crowd of people standing around the sets—firefighters, police officers, people in overalls and hard hats like us. We moved in close enough to hear.

"This enemy attacked not just our people, but all freedom-loving people everywhere in the world. The United States of America will use all our resources to conquer this enemy. We will rally the world. The battle will take time and resolve. But make no mistake about it: we will win."

There was a rumble of people agreeing with him.

"The freedom-loving nations of the world stand by our side. This will be a monumental struggle of good versus evil. But good will prevail. Thank you very much."

The president walked away from the podium, and everybody, including James and me, burst into applause. The clapping stung my hand. Somehow, in the middle of all this, knowing what I knew, having seen what I'd seen, this was what I needed to hear.

"James, is that you?"

I looked over. There was a firefighter standing a few feet away. His face was covered in a thick layer of grime and soot, hiding his features.

"Yeah?" James said. His expression indicated that maybe the man knew him, but James didn't know who he was.

"It's me, Charlie. Charlie O'Leary."

"Mr. O'Leary . . . I didn't recognize you . . . sorry," James said.

"That's okay. I hardly recognized you, either. Haven't seen you in about a year, since that firefighters' picnic. You probably recognize a lot of the other guys here. Every firefighter in the city is down here. I didn't expect to see you, though."

"We came down to help," James said.

"Your father," he said. "He's . . ."

"He's missing."

"He's with Ladder Fourteen, right?"

James nodded.

"The whole crew is missing," Mr. O'Leary said.

"I didn't know," James said. "I just know about my father."

"And your mother?" he asked.

"She's at home."

"Does she know you're down here?"

James shook his head.

"How old are you, James? You can't be any older than sixteen."

I wondered if he was going to try to lie to him.

"Fifteen. I'm only fifteen."

"You really shouldn't be down here at all. You're too young. Especially if your mother doesn't know, and—"

"I *have* to be here. Please don't make me leave. Please," James begged.

Mr. O'Leary reached down and put a hand on his shoulder. "James, we firefighters always say we're like family. You know that."

James nodded.

"And those aren't just words. We are family. All of us. The men on the line and the wives and kids we leave behind each day when we go to work. One big family."

"That's how my father sees it."

"That's how we all see it. What do you think your father would say to you if he were standing right here? Would he want you to be down here or safe at home?"

James didn't answer, which I guess *was* an answer. This was perfect. This guy was going to force James to leave—force us to leave; I wouldn't have to tell anybody or do anything, the decision would now be out of my hands.

"I know this is where you want to be. I know this is where you think your father would want you to be. But it isn't. There are thousands of us down here to do this job, but only you can do the job you need to do."

There was a pause and I waited for him to continue. What job was that?

"I've known your mother for almost as long as I've known your father. She's one of the nicest people you'd ever want to meet. Right now she's at home, still thinking that your father is going to walk in the door, isn't she?"

James nodded his head ever so slightly.

"But you and I know the truth. There have been no rescues since this morning. We've moved from rescue to recovery—from trying to find people to trying to find bodies."

I saw a small shiver run through James.

"You need to go home. Your mother shouldn't be alone."

"She isn't alone."

"She needs *you* to be there." He took James by both shoulders and looked him square in the eyes. "I could make you leave, have you taken from the site, but I'm not going to do that, James."

"Thanks."

Why not? I felt like yelling out.

"I know you just want to help, try to make a difference, like your father. Your old man was a great firefighter and a good man."

Was—past tense—as in, *He's gone, no more.*

"I know," James said.

"You decide what you have to do. I know you'll make the right choice," Mr. O'Leary said. "Now, I have to get back out and do *my* job." He turned and walked away.

James and I stood there in silence. I tried to think

what I should say to him, but I just didn't know.

"I'm not stupid," James said.

"What?"

"I'm not stupid. I know . . . my father . . . he's . . . he's dead."

"So . . . what are we going to do now?" I asked.

"It's time for us to go home," he said. "My mother needs me."

CHAPTER
FOURTEEN

The train rumbled along the tracks. James stared out the window. He hadn't said more than a half-dozen words since we'd left the site. We'd turned in our construction boots and goggles and gloves—well, at least James's gloves. Mine were so bloody they just got tossed in the garbage, along with our masks. We'd then washed up as best we could with the limited water available. We actually still looked as though we were wearing goggles and masks, because the places they'd covered were the only areas that were clean . . . or at least cleaner.

The only part of me that was completely clean was

my left hand. The doctor had scoured it and disinfected it and then put in a few new stitches to replace the one that had popped and a couple that were loose. My hand was still tingling.

We were the only two people on our car. The few other people who had boarded at Grand Central had exited already. We hadn't bought tickets. I still had the note from the conductor, but nobody had even asked. The only people who had checked us were the soldiers when we'd entered Grand Central. We told them where we'd been and what we'd been doing and they told us how they wished they could be down there helping. I wanted to tell them not to wish for something they really didn't want, but in the end I kept my thoughts to myself.

I wasn't surprised that nobody had asked for our tickets. Nobody seemed to care about things like that right now. Everybody seemed to be in the same dazed state we were in. That's how I felt. Dazed. Numb. Unfeeling. I just wished I could stop thinking completely.

"Have you decided what you're going to tell your parents?" James asked.

That startled me out of my thoughts. "I guess I'm going to tell them the truth."

"Your mother is going to freak."

"Probably. But I think she should know—they both should know. I think that maybe my father will understand."

"You think so?"

"I hope. I went down there because you wanted me to, but I think I needed to go there for me, as well."

"You had to see that the monster was really dead."

I smiled. "Yeah, I did. My father will understand that. Besides, unless I'm stopping at your place for a shower it's going to be pretty obvious when they see me that I wasn't just walking around the neighborhood."

"I guess you're right."

"I'm guessing, once my mother sees me and knows I'm fine, it won't be so bad."

"Is that why you haven't turned your phone back on?" he asked.

"My phone! I forgot!"

I reached into my pocket, pulled it out, and turned it on. It searched for a signal and then told me I had four missed calls. I didn't need to check to see who those were from.

"It would be better to talk to her in person. We'll be there soon enough."

We were only two stops away from ours.

"How about you?" I asked. "Are you going to tell your mom?"

He nodded. "The truth is painful sometimes, but you have to tell it . . . and live it."

I knew what he meant. There was no point in living a lie, or living in denial. She needed to realize what everybody else already knew . . . no matter how painful it was.

"You ever get mad at your father?" James asked.

"All the time. I get mad when he acts as though work is more important than us. It makes me angry that he's gone so much."

"I'd get mad at my old man, too."

"But your father always spent a lot of time with you."

"It wasn't about time. It was about what he did when he wasn't with me, with us. What he did for a living." He paused. "My mother always says that police officers and firefighters are like little boys."

I didn't understand what that meant, but I'd heard her say it . . . I'd heard her say it *today*. Was that really today? It seemed like a week ago that my mother and I had visited their house.

"Did you ever want to be a cop or a fireman when you were growing up?" James asked.

"I guess everybody does at one time, when they're a kid."

"Yeah, but most people grow out of it. Some don't. My mom says that bad little boys become police officers and good little boys become firefighters. My father was like a good little boy. He was always there to play road hockey or shoot hoops, or to hang around, or to help shovel the neighbor's driveway. He was like a little boy who never grew up. Sometimes I wish he *had* grown up."

"And sometimes I wish my father hadn't grown up so much," I said.

"I guess it's part of human nature to want something different from what you have. Your father is a businessman. When he goes to work every day do you ever worry about whether or not he'll be coming home?"

"Not really . . . although maybe I should."

"Things happen to everybody. Maybe not like what happened yesterday, but bad things, like car accidents, things you can't control. But for a firefighter there's nothing but bad things. So maybe it's his dream, but it isn't the dream of his family. All we want is for him to come home. He goes out every day, and the people he leaves behind know what could happen. Do you know which profession has the highest rate of job-related deaths?"

"Isn't it like that TV show, those fishermen in Alaska who catch crabs?" I asked.

"I'm talking *real* jobs, the kind that people here do," he snapped, and I instantly felt bad. "It's firefighters. When you're little you think your father is the greatest, strongest, most powerful man in the world."

"That's he's bulletproof," I said, using the word James had used for me.

"Yeah, that he's bulletproof, that nothing can happen to him. But then you get older and you know better. And then you hear about other firefighters who have died in the line of duty. People you've never heard of, or people your father knew. Then it's a family friend, somebody like that man today, Charlie O'Leary. You've met the guy at a picnic or a Christmas party or something, and then you hear that he's gone, died in the line of duty. And then it's not just one or two, but more. And you start thinking that every time your dad goes to work might be the last time you ever see him."

"That would be brutal."

"He puts on that uniform, pats you on the head, gives everybody a hug, and leaves, and you know that he's risking his life for people he doesn't even know, and he's leaving behind a family who's scared. But we have to pretend we're not scared, right? I remember so many times my mother would listen to the news and hear about a fire. She'd make some phone calls to try to figure out if his company was involved. And then she'd slip off into the bathroom, and later she'd come out smiling. But I could tell she'd been in tears, because she'd heard that it was his company and he was there. She'd put on a big, fake smile for us so we wouldn't worry."

"Like she's doing now?" I asked.

He nodded. "And when he didn't come home when he was supposed to she'd get even more fake-happy, to try to stop us from worrying. But I knew."

"And is that when you'd get mad at him?" I asked.

"Yeah. Really mad. I wanted to know why he couldn't get a real job, like your father or everybody else's father I know!"

I chuckled. "You know, there isn't one kid we hang with who didn't think that your father had the coolest job in the world, that he wasn't the coolest father around."

James smiled. A sad little smile. "He was pretty cool."

There was that word again—*was*, past tense. Gone.

The train pulled into the station. This was sort of like perfect timing. I didn't know what else I could say. We climbed off the train and walked along the platform, exiting out onto the street. James's house was in one direction and mine was in the other.

"I guess this is it," he said.

I wanted to get home, but I wondered if maybe I should walk with him to his house.

"I know the way," he said, reading my mind. "I think I can find it myself."

"Sure . . . okay . . . I know."

He reached out, wrapped his arms around me, and gave me a hug. I hugged him back. "I really appreciate your coming with me," he said.

"Thanks for bringing me along. Like I said, it wasn't just for you."

"Thanks for saying that. I'll talk to you later."

"For sure. Call me if you need to talk . . . okay?"

"Okay." His expression got serious. "I'm not mad at him any more, you know, in case you were thinking that. I haven't been for a long time. I got older and realized that the world needs people who run into those buildings while everybody else is running out. And I know that he was doing it not just because he was a little boy who didn't grow up, but because the world needs men who are willing to risk their lives, even for strangers . . . *Especially* for strangers."

"Like yesterday," I said quietly.

I thought about his father climbing those stairs, heading up toward the fire as we were running in the opposite direction. And I remembered how he looked—like there was no other place in the world he would have chosen to be, even if he could.

"Yeah, like yesterday. He went there to help people, and that's what made him feel good, feel alive. And I wouldn't have made him stop even if I could have, because that's the core of who he was, everything I know about him, everything I love about him. I realized at some point that being a firefighter wasn't just what he *did*, it's what he *was*."

"I understand," I said.

"I thought you might. I just hope *my* kids understand."

"Your kids? You still want to be a firefighter?"

"We need people who are willing to help other people, who are willing to run into burning buildings, who are willing to risk their lives. Maybe we need them now more than ever. We were down there, just a couple of guys, part of hundreds, maybe thousands of people trying to help. We weren't alone. We worked together, and we stood together. Because, the way I see it, united we stand and divided we fall."

CHAPTER
FIFTEEN

My phone rang. Three guesses who that was. I flipped it open.

"Hey, Mom."

"Will! I've been calling you for the last three hours and you haven't answered!" she shrieked. "Do you know how worried I've been? Where have you been?"

"The more important question is, Where am I now?"

"What?"

"I'm three houses down. I'll be home in less than a minute. Can we talk when I get there?"

"You bet your life we're going to be talking. Do you know how worried I am or—"

"Let's talk in person." I hung up on her. She wouldn't like that, but how much more angry was she going to be, either way?

I turned up our walkway and the front door opened. My mother was standing there.

"I just wanted to say how sorry I am."

"We were so worried about you . . . Your face," she gasped. "What happened to you?"

"It's nothing. It's just—"

"Were you in a fight?"

"A fight?"

"Did you and James get in a fight?"

"Don't be ridiculous. James and I have never fought each other in our entire—"

"Not with each other. Did you two get into a fight with somebody else?" she demanded.

"No!" I protested. "Why would you even think that we'd been in a fight?"

"Look at your face!"

"It wasn't a fight. It was a—"

"Because with males, grief and sadness often lead to anger."

I was starting to feel angry, but that had more to do with what she was saying and what she wasn't letting me say. I could have snapped out something nasty, but I just took a deep breath instead. There was no point in reacting. I was already going to be in enough trouble.

"Well, don't you have anything to say for yourself?" she questioned.

"I already said I was sorry I made you worry."

"Sorry isn't good enough. This time you've really—"

"How about," I said, cutting *her* off this time, "I tell you what happened, and why I'm so late? Would you like that?"

"Of course. That's all I want."

"Then could we go inside, please, instead of doing this on the front step?"

It was like all of a sudden she realized where we were standing. She ushered me in and closed the door.

"It's not just your face, Will. You're filthy all over," she said.

"I am filthy, but I'm home. I'm here, and I *am* sorry. I really don't like worrying you."

I wrapped my arms around her. She was shaky—or was it me?—and as she hugged me back she started to sob.

"I'm really, really sorry," I said quietly in her ear.

"Will?"

It was my father. I looked up at him, and when he saw my face his expression registered the shock I expected.

"What happened to you?" He sounded more than a little worried too.

"Can we sit down?" I asked. "My legs are pretty tired."

"You should be tired after all that walking you've been doing," he said.

"We weren't just walking. Let me explain."

I sat down in the wing chair, and my parents sat on the sofa across from me. In the corner the big TV was on, sound off, CNN and Ground Zero on the screen. Now that I'd seen it myself in person, the TV image seemed even more real.

"Well?" my mother prompted.

Now that I had their attention I had to figure out where I should start. In a way it didn't matter. I was going to be in trouble no matter where I began this story.

"I was with James all afternoon," I finally began. "He needed me."

"And how is James doing?" my father asked.

"I think about as well as he can be."

"And you said you were doing more than just walking," my father said.

This was where the trouble began. I nodded my head. "We started out walking, and we found ourselves down by the train station."

"And you went into New York," my father said quietly.

"Yes." I wasn't expecting him to know that.

"But why would you two go into New York?" my mother asked.

"We *had* to go."

"The whole city is closed down. Why would you possibly have to go New York? Where did you go?"

"Ground Zero," my father said before I could answer.

"What?" It was as though my mother had heard him but couldn't believe her ears. "Is your father right?"

"Yes," I said, my voice hardly louder than a whisper.

My mother shook her head vigorously. "No, no, you couldn't do that . . . you wouldn't . . . Why would you want to do that?" She sounded completely confused, but also frightened.

It would have been simpler, easier, to just blame it all on James, tell her it had all been his idea, but that wasn't true. In some way, actually, it had been my *mother's* idea.

"It was because of something you talked to me about," I said to her.

"Me? What could I possibly have said that would make you think you had to go into the city?"

"You told me that sometimes people need to see the body to know that somebody is really dead."

"I said that?"

"Yeah. Like with Grandpa's funeral and the open casket."

"I think I understand," my father said. "James needed to go to Ground Zero to see what happened to his father."

"Yeah, but it wasn't just him. I needed to go down there as well. *I* needed to see it."

"*You* needed to stay home," my mother said.

"No," I said. "You needed me to stay home, Mom, but I needed to go."

"That still doesn't explain how you got so dirty. What were you doing that would cause you to get so filthy?"

I took another deep breath. This wasn't going to go over well. "We didn't just go down to look. We were helping."

"Helping? Helping how?"

I pointed at the TV. There on the screen was the site, people moving around, cranes removing giant girders, and the bucket-brigade lines.

"James and I were doing that."

"What?" she gasped.

"We were on the site, helping to remove debris. They gave us helmets, masks, gloves, and even construction boots, and we helped to—"

"I can't believe what I'm hearing," my mother said.

"We needed to do it," I said. "We needed to try to help."

"Who in their right minds would let two fifteen-year-old boys—?"

"We told them we were eighteen," I said.

"Eighteen? Who would believe that?"

"I don't know if they really did believe us," I admitted. "But they heard about James's father, and they knew we needed to be there."

"I understand," my father said.

"You do?" my mother asked.

"If I hadn't had to do what I was doing today, I would have gone down myself," my father said.

"But . . . but . . . even if you *had* gone down you would have told me you were going," my mother argued.

"Of course."

"But if *I'd* told you what I was going to do, you wouldn't have let *me* go, would you?" I asked.

"Of course I wouldn't have let you go . . . I . . .

I . . ." She looked from me to my father and then back to me. "You're right. I just wish I understood why this matters so much."

"It was something else you said, about denial," I explained. "Going there made me understand how close I came—we came—to dying. And you were right. I guess it does mean something different when the bullet just whizzes past your head."

She knew what I was referring to, even if my father was confused.

"I'm not denying anything," I told her.

She gave me a little smile. "I have to admit that even if I had known the reason I still wouldn't have let you go . . . at least, not by yourself."

"I wasn't by myself. I was with James. And James and I were with hundreds of other people, all trying to help, all trying to do whatever we could."

"But if I'd known, I would have driven you boys down myself," she said.

"You would have?" Now I was surprised.

"I don't really understand all of this," she said, "and maybe it's part of my own denial to even try. I was just so scared, so terrified of what might have happened, and it's the last place in the world that I'd want to be, but I'm starting to understand how important this was for you." She turned to my father. "Important for *both* of you. I don't really like it, but I'll understand if you two need to go to Ground Zero tomorrow."

I shook my head. "I'm okay. I think I've seen what

I needed to see. But I'll go if you need me to," I said to my father. "I'd go with you."

"Not tomorrow, but I think it is important at some point for us to go there. I think we need to see what we survived. Not just to watch it on TV, but to see it with our own eyes." He turned to my mother. "I think all *three* of us need to go. After all, it wasn't just the two of us who survived this tragedy."

He reached out and put an arm around my mother, and she curled into his side. She buried her head in his shoulder and started to quietly cry. My father's eyes were all red, and I could tell that he was fighting to hold back tears. I was too.

"Thousands of lives were ended yesterday," my father said. "And tens of thousands of other lives were broken or altered beyond recognition. The lives of people like the Bennetts. And for the hundreds of millions of people who make up this country, life has changed. We don't even know how much or in what ways, or how this is all going to affect us, but things will never be the same again. That much I'm sure of."

I thought about it. When I'd woken up that morning I'd wanted desperately to believe that everything would just go back to normal, that my life would be what it had been two days before. Now I knew that wasn't possible, that my father was right. We'd somehow dodged the bullet, but it had still changed who we were, and that change could never be undone.

"These people—these monsters—who did this, they

thought that if they could bring down those buildings they could bring down our country," my father said. "They just don't understand *who* we are—*what* we are." He paused. "This country is strong, and our people are strong. Our government will find the men responsible and make them pay. Have no doubt."

"I don't, but *we* need to do something, too."

"You did something today, and I'm proud of you."

"We're both proud of you," my mother said.

"I did what I needed to do."

"That's what we're all going to do," my father said. "We're going to go back to work; planes will start flying again; we'll go back to our lives. We're not going to forget what happened, or the people who have died, but we're going to honor their lives by continuing to live ours. We're going to come together, fight together, and stand together."

"United we stand," I said.

My father smiled. "United we stand," he agreed.

ABOUT THE AUTHOR

Eric Walters, a former elementary school teacher, began writing as a way of to encourage his students to become more enthusiastic about literature. in their own creative work. His first novel was set in his school with six of his students as characters. His young adult books have won numerous awards, including the Silver Birch, Blue Heron, Red Maple, Snow Willow, and Ruth Schwartz. He lives in Mississauga, Ontario. His website is www.ericwalters.net.